The Slaughtered Virgin of Zenopolis

The 1st Case for Inspector Capstan

David Blake

www.david-blake.com

Edited and proofread by Lorraine Swoboda

Cover design by David Blake

Published in Great Britain, 2016

Disclaimer:
These are works of fiction. Names, characters, businesses, places, events and incidents are either the products of the author's imagination or used in a fictitious manner. Any resemblance to actual persons, living or dead, or actual events is purely coincidental.

Copyright © David Blake 2016
The right of David Blake to be identified as the Author of the Work has been asserted by him in accordance with the Copyright, Designs and Patents Act 1998. All rights reserved. This book is for your enjoyment only. No part of this publication may be reproduced, distributed, or transmitted in any form or by any means, including photocopying, recording, or other electronic or mechanical methods, without the prior written permission of the copyright owner except in the case of brief quotations embodied in critical reviews and certain other non-commercial uses permitted by copyright law.

All rights reserved.

ISBN: 152283477X
ISBN-13: 978-1522834779

DEDICATION

For Akiko, Akira and Kai.

THE INSPECTOR CAPSTAN
SERIES INCLUDES:

1. The Slaughtered Virgin of Zenopolis
2. The Curious Case of Cut-Throat Cate
3. The Thrills & Spills of Genocide Jill

CONTENTS

	Acknowledgments	i
1	I'm trying to give a tour here	1
2	I think my Mum might have one	9
3	Just who the hell do you think you are?	22
4	Question time	42
5	The Roman Baths	49
6	Eat, drink and be merry	61
7	A kitchen with a view	73
8	The lady's not for ogling	87
9	Fight another day	98
10	I'd look good on you	103
11	Invasive rabbits	110
12	Well, it's the funniest thing	119
13	Handcuffs and washing machines	132
14	Got it	139
15	Cloud Watching	145
16	To fall or not to fall	151
17	All hands, all hands	153
18	I'm not dead	159

19	Happy Bath Day	163
20	Stilettos, size five	168
21	Ground rules	173
22	The front page headline	175
23	Council of War	180
24	Roman Day	191
25	The Senate and People of Rome	196
26	A decent game	207
27	The Ides of August	216
28	How are you?	223
29	Casualties of War	228
30	Can you hear me?	232
31	Isn't that right?	234
32	What is truth?	240
33	Which is what had to be proven	251

ACKNOWLEDGMENTS

I'd like to thank my family for putting up with me and my rather odd sense of humour.

I'd also like to thank my Editor and Proofreader, Lorraine Swoboda, for making sure that what I write makes sense, sort of, and that all the words are in the right order.

CHAPTER I
QUAE EGO PRAECIPIO SPECTATUM IRENT
I'm trying to give a tour here

'OK, EVERYONE, please stop there and look over to your right.'

Having all been staring at either their guide books or their smartphones, the untidy group of tourists walked into the back of each other, prompting a brief round of apologies in a variety of different languages.

'On the far wall you'll see a large fresco depicting the scene of Roman Citizens enjoying the public bathing rooms, right here at Bath's famous Basin Museum.'

They peered over at the rather tired-looking work of art.

'It's thought to have been painted by Clumptius Reginius,' the Tour Guide continued, 'the son of Perinius Reginius, a Senator of Rome itself.'

'How do you spell "Clumptius"?' asked a young girl with a German accent, taking notes at the front of the group.

'Excuse me?' asked a tall man at the back who sounded more Eastern European. 'Is that man supposed to be down there?'

'I'm sorry, but can we keep our questions to the

end, please? We have a lot to get through and I really need to be at the bank by one.'

It wasn't even the end of her first part-time job of the day, but Becky Philips had already had enough. She was only doing it, and all the others she had, because her parents refused to pay her way through university, but the whole "work" thing was all rather tedious and being a Tour Guide for Bath's virtually unknown Basin Museum was the worst of the lot.

'So anyway,' she continued, 'as I was saying…'

'But he really doesn't look very well,' said the tall man at the back again, looking down to his left, instead of to the right, and pointing at a security guard lying face up at the bottom of one of the empty ancient basins.

'Oh, I'm sure he's fine,' she said, absently. 'Now if we can all look over to the right again…'

'But he's got blood coming out of his head!'

'Excuse me, sir, but would you mind not interrupting me all the time? I'm trying to give a tour here!'

'And what looks like a sword sticking out of his chest.'

By this time everyone in the group was looking the wrong way, down at the man splayed out at the bottom of the basin, with blood seeping from his head, and a Roman sword sticking out of his chest.

Becky glanced at the body and back to the group again. At this rate she wasn't even going to have time for a sandwich.

'Honestly, everyone, I'm sure he's OK. The security guards are always up to something strange. He's probably doing a training exercise.'

Most of the group mumbled in agreement and went back to looking at the fresco again.

'I'm sorry, Miss, but it looks to me like he's been attacked, or even murdered. I really think you should call the police, or at least an ambulance.'

'Fine!'

Having given up all hope of having lunch, she looked back down at the security guard. On closer observation, she had to agree with the man at the back; he didn't look too good. She knew nothing about medicine; she was studying Business, but if pushed on the subject she'd have to say that the man did look as if he was dead, especially given the fact that he did indeed have a Roman sword sticking out of him and a large amount of blood surrounding his head.

'I'll call for someone,' she said, and turned around to shout, 'JEFFREY? JEFFREY!' Not hearing a response she really hollered out, 'JEFFREY!!!'

A moment later, Jeffrey Hetheringshaw, Senior Curator of the Basin Museum, came hobbling out from the lobby.

'Yes, yes, yes, I'm coming, I'm coming. Now, what is it?'

'There's a body down there,' she said, pointing at it.

'Oh, I see, yes. Hold on.'

Jeffrey carefully detached the red cord that cordoned off the empty Roman Basin, and which normally stopped people from falling into it, and tentatively approached the edge of what looked to the uninitiated like a decrepit, quarter-sized indoor swimming pool. He leaned forward, cupped his hands around his mouth and called out, 'Excuse me, but I really don't think you're supposed to be down there!'

'For God's sake Jeffrey, he's dead!' said Becky, folding her arms and looking at her watch.

'Oh, do you think so?' he asked, turning around.

'Er, yes, Jeffrey, he's definitely dead. He's got a sword sticking out of him, for Christ's sake!'

'Yes, I see that now.'

He really didn't, but never liked to admit that he could hardly see his own coffee at break time, let alone anything beyond the length of his arms.

'I suppose I'd better call for an ambulance then.'

The tall man at the back spoke up again.

'Personally, I think you should call the police. It looks to me like he's been attacked, and as he's a security guard, it may be that you were robbed last night.'

'You're right, young man!'

The man wasn't young at all, but he let it go.

'I'll call for the police men people,' Jeffrey continued. 'You'd all better wait here until they arrive. They may need to ask you some questions.'

Becky was losing her patience. There was absolutely no way she was going to stand there for another hour surrounded by a bunch of brainless tourists and an equally moronic group of policemen, as they asked her a series of stupid and ultimately pointless questions.

'Look, Jeffrey, couldn't we just ignore it for now? He's not going anywhere and I'm sure the police have got better things to do than attend to what's probably just been a nasty accident.'

'Well, I don't know. Amie, isn't it?'

'No, it's Becky!'

'Sorry, Becky, but if the man has been attacked and stabbed then we really should call for the police men.'

The crowd mumbled their approval again; after all, this was proving to be much more entertaining than what they'd first expected from a tour of the Roman Basin Museum.

Becky had to think fast. At this rate she'd not only lose her lunch break but also be late starting her next job at the bank.

'But Jeffrey, if we get the police involved in a murder inquiry it's going to attract a huge amount of bad publicity for us. They'd also have to close us down for weeks on end as they do all their forensic investigation stuff, and right in the middle of our peak tourist season, which would put a real dent in our expected income for the year.'

Jeffrey turned around to look at this girl, as best he could anyway, with real interest. She was much more intelligent than he'd first thought, and he could certainly do with someone like her helping out around the place a little more.

'You're absolutely right, my dear! Now...' he swivelled around to look at the group as a whole, 'does anyone have any ideas as to how we can hide the body of this poor man who must simply have had a nasty fall?'

The tour group all looked around at each other.

'I suppose you could fill it up with water,' suggested the tall man at the back.

Everyone turned around to stare at him. It was just such a good idea!

'Yes, but wouldn't the body then float to the surface?' asked the German girl, not so easily impressed.

'She's right, I'm afraid,' said Jeffrey, nodding his

head.

'But what if we could weigh him down first?' the tall man proposed.

Becky spoke up, 'Yes, that's it! There are loads of old statues around here. We could simply push one on top of him and then just fill the basin up with water. Nobody would be any the wiser!'

'Well, yes,' Jeffrey spoke again, 'but which statue could we use?'

'Does it matter?' Becky asked. 'They're all the bloody same, aren't they?'

'I suppose some of them are a little similar.'

Jeffrey didn't think any of them were the same at all, and found the very idea to be deeply offensive. However, he was a practical man and understood the importance of being able to hide the body as quickly as possible, certainly before the next group of tourists came through and most definitely before the police got wind of it.

After scratching his head for a few moments he said, 'I suppose we could use the Slaughtered Virgin of Zenopolis, out in the lobby.'

Having made up his mind, he pushed his way through the group, towards the entrance hall.

'Follow me, everyone. I'll need your help if we're going to carry it.'

The whole group, including Becky, looked at each other, shrugged, and followed on after him.

About five minutes later, they came staggering back carrying the statue of the Slaughtered Virgin of Zenopolis. Jeffrey was leading the way, the tall man was carrying the statue's feet, Becky had its head and everyone else just gathered around the sides offering moral support more than anything else.

When the statue was parallel to the edge of the basin, Jeffrey raised his arm.

'Right, hold it there.'

'But how are we going to get it onto the body?' asked the German student.

'Can't we just throw it on?' the tall man urged, breathing hard.

'Yes, I'm sure we can just chuck it on top of him,' Becky said, beginning to think she may have time for lunch after all. 'On three,' she said, re-taking command of her group. 'And one, and two, and THREE!'

With that, they flung the naked virgin down on top of the security guard where she landed with a loud squelch.

'Good shot everyone!' said Jeffrey, clearly impressed with the athleticism of today's youth.

They all gazed back down. The Slaughtered Virgin of Zenopolis now looked more like the Roman Temptress of Saducia, who'd just enjoyed excessive copulation with a Celtic Marauder, before running him through with his own sword.

'I think that looks quite good!' said Becky, enjoying herself. 'Maybe we can leave it like that.'

'But his blood has spattered out everywhere!' said the tall man, who'd taken up his regular place at the back of the group. 'I really think we'd best fill it up with water, just to be safe.'

'Yes, quite right,' piped up Jeffrey again. 'I'll fetch a hose. There's one around the corner.' And off he shuffled.

Becky glanced at her watch again. 'I can still make it,' she said to herself, and raced after him to lend a hand.

Moments later they returned pulling a dark grey fire hose behind them. Reaching the edge, they dropped it in and Becky scurried back to turn on the tap. She rejoined the group as they watched the water spread out over the ancient floor.

'That will take a while to fill up,' said Jeffrey. 'I think I'd best cordon off this basin again until it does. Thank you, everyone. I suppose you can all be on your way now.'

'Is it OK if I head off as well?' asked Becky, trying not to appear too desperate.

'Oh, er, is that the time already? Yes, of course my dear, and thank you again for your help.'

As soon as the words had left his mouth she was off, pushing and shoving her way through the tour group, heading out towards the entrance. It was going to be tight, but she might just make it.

CHAPTER II
PUTO MUM HABERENT
I think my Mum might have one

HEADING STRAIGHT out onto York Street, Becky glanced at her watch again. She was late after all, and she wasn't happy about it. She really didn't like being late. She'd always been an "on-time" sort of a girl. That was her thing. Actually, being early was more her thing. She did find it difficult to be on time without being early first; and because she was always on time, she found herself being early rather a lot. For her, being early was an unfortunate by-product of being on time. It was the only way she could guarantee arriving at her destination exactly when she said she would; and although she did find arriving early somewhat annoying, at least it wasn't stressful; whereas being late was, which is why she preferred to be early, rather than late.

A few years before, she decided that she'd had enough of being early all the time and just wanted to be, like everyone else; so she had a go at being late on purpose. However, she soon discovered that deliberately trying to be late was even more stressful than actually being so, and gave up, accepting the fact that she was just one of those people who didn't "do" late, not on purpose at any rate.

But after throwing the Slaughtered Virgin of

Zenopolis on top of the dead security guard who lay at the bottom of an empty Roman Basin with a sword sticking out of him, before filling it up with water to hide it long enough for her to make it to the bank on time, she was now late, and it wasn't on purpose. At the rate she was going she'd be lucky if she had time to pick up something to eat. So she decided to turn immediately left out of the museum and left again, to walk straight past Bath Abbey. There she danced around the normal eclectic mix of tourists, before popping out onto Cheap Street, over to High Street and then into CoffeeRoast to join the queue for her usual Cottage Cheese Sandwich.

If she'd had more time, she'd have turned right out of the museum's entrance to head for Stall Street, and the CoffeeBeans at the end - she preferred CoffeeBeans - but the Instathon Bank was only a few doors down from CoffeeRoast, and going straight past the Abbey shaved off around three minutes walking time.

Having finally battled her way to the front of the queue, she considered that ordering a coffee was definitely pushing it, so she just grabbed a sandwich and, with no time to eat it, stuffed it deep inside her somewhat generously proportioned handbag and turned left to the bank.

With pure determination and some well-timed sidesteps, she made it with just thirty seconds to spare and attempted to heave open its heavy, glass door. But at that exact moment, three young men wearing brown warehouse overalls arrived and also attempted to pull open the door. However, the process of four people now trying to open the same door, at the same time, was making a relatively simple task somewhat over-complex. And just as they were about to successfully get it open, the men all decided that they needed to pull black ski-masks over their heads, causing the door to close again, and leaving Becky to wait with a level of patience she didn't know she possessed. Finally, when they had finished their somewhat unusual mask adornment routine, the four of them started the process of pulling open the door all over again, and as soon as it was wide enough, they all burst in, looking like a group auditioning for the latest Guy Ritchie film.

Becky was first to do something and waved at her line manager standing behind the reception desk to signal her arrival. This prompted the three men to pull out their sawn-off shotguns and wave them about, to signal theirs. The shorter of the three bank robbers then shouted, 'GET YOUR HANDS IN THE AIR! THIS IS A ROBBERY!'

He'd been practising that line for ages in front of his mirror at home, and thought he'd delivered it to perfection. He was aiming for something that would be loud enough to be heard, but not so loud that everyone would start panicking. Unfortunately for him, the sight of three men bursting into a bank wearing brown overalls and black ski masks and brandishing sawn-off shotguns bore such a close resemblance to the film "Lock, Stock and Two Smoking Barrels" that there was only ever going to be one reaction, no matter what he said, or how he said it.

So, as everyone started screaming and grabbing hold of each other, the shorter one was forced to reflect on the fact that he must have over-cooked it somehow. The other two seemed to agree with him, and they all just stood about, surveying the room, trying to understand how it was possible for a group of civilised, educated and upright Human Beings to degenerate quite so quickly into a species who'd lost the gift of coherent speech and who were unable to remain standing without the support of the person next to them.

Becky was probably the only person in the entire bank who wasn't either blubbering or holding on to someone. In fact she was feeling more hungry than scared, and was thinking about the sandwich in her bag more than the armed robbers in the bank. She was also now desperate for a coffee, and was regretting not having ordered one earlier, especially now that her line manager seemed to be preoccupied by the current events and probably wouldn't have noticed even if she had been a few minutes late.

But as she stood there, with her hands in the air, thinking about the uneaten sandwich in her bag and the un-ordered coffee in the shop, nothing else seemed to be happening. The customers continued to cuddle each other whilst forgetting that they were supposed to have their hands in the air, the three cashiers behind the security glass seemed to be doing something very similar, her line manager at the reception desk had started to sob but had at least remembered to keep her hands up, and the bank robbers just stood there gawping and waving their guns around in a vaguely threatening way.

To help move things along a little, Becky called over to the cashiers, who were looking more like air stewardesses weighing up their options after watching the wings fall off their transatlantic jumbo jet.

'Trisha? Trisha! Hello, Trisha! Can you get Brian please? I really think he should be dealing with this.'

Hearing someone speak without permission, the three criminals rotated their guns around to level them at Becky's head, leaving her little choice but to offer an explanation for her unsolicited outburst.

'I think we need to get Brian. He's the Bank Manager. He's probably the best person for you to talk to, given the circumstances.'

They all nodded in agreement and rotated their guns back to face the mass of cowering customers, which only seemed to encourage another rendition of their un-rehearsed performance of Scream Two, The Musical, forcing the shorter bank robber to raise his voice more than he'd have like to.

'OK, yes, can someone please get the Bank Manager for us?'

He was looking straight at the three cashiers, who'd all started pointing at themselves, and then at each other, as they tried to work out which one he meant. Sensing their confusion, he clarified his command with, 'You, the girl with the dark hair.'

As all three of them had the same colour hair, they continued to point at themselves and then at each other.

'The one with the big earrings,' but they all had quite large earrings, so this really didn't help.

Eventually he gave up trying to be subtle and said, 'The fat one in the middle!'

He didn't like to be offensive but as they all wore the same uniforms, had the same colour hair, and all had similar sized earrings, it was really difficult to verbally distinguish between the three of them.

Now even more upset than she was before, the fat one started to sob and ran to disappear through the door at the back.

'Right, now calm down everyone. As long as you all do as you're told, nobody's going to get hurt.'

This belated effort to placate his audience did seem to offer some comfort, and the crying dissipated into more of an undulating series of moans and whimpers.

'May I put my hands down now?' Becky asked, as she began to feel the weight of them hanging over her head. 'I really can't hold them up like this forever.'

'Er, yes, all right. Everyone can put their hands down now; as long as nobody moves!'

The assembled audience were forced to assume that the phrase "as long as nobody moves" didn't include their hands, so all those who'd remembered to keep their hands up, now brought them down; and all those who hadn't, thought they'd better put them up first, before bringing them straight down again. But by the time they'd put them up and down, they couldn't remember what they were supposed to do and considered putting them up again to ask, but thought better of it.

'Is it OK if I eat my sandwich now?' Becky was starving. 'I do work here you know,' she added. 'I was just a little late, and I didn't have time for lunch.'

It was an unexpected question, and the bank robbers were forced to confer before the shorter one answered, 'Yes, all right, but no funny business!'

Becky wasn't sure what he meant by that. She'd never been funny in her life. Even when she was drunk she struggled to tell a joke; but she was grateful for the chance to eat, and pulled out her Cottage Cheese

Sandwich to begin the rather noisy task of removing its shrink-wrapping.

Just as she managed her very first bite, a chubby bald man squeezed his fat little head out from the back office, probably hoping that the cashier, who'd only just finished blubbering out what was happening, had either made the whole thing up or had at least exaggerated it, as she was prone to. But unfortunately for him she hadn't, and seeing that the situation was exactly as she'd described, he walked slowly out, raising both his hands.

'Now everyone p-p-please remain calm,' he said, with a thin, small voice that quivered like a leaf hanging off a dead tree. 'My name's Brian Haverlington. I'm the Bank Manager here at the Instathon Bank in this, the historic City of Bath.'

Sounding like Becky doing her "tour-guide" thing, he inched his way towards the security door that separated the cashiers' area from where the customers queued. Keeping one hand raised he dropped the other to enter the combination before opening it.

'Right, we want all the money out here in bags in exactly…' the shorter one stalled and consulted with his two accomplices, '… ten… no… five… yes, five minutes.'

Having made their decision, they reinforced it by waving their shotguns around again.

'Yes, of course,' said Brian, feeling more confident now that he'd established a dialogue. 'Do any of you have an account with us?' It was a question he was used to asking whenever someone wanted to make a cash withdrawal.

Somewhat surprised, the bank robbers glanced

around at each other before the middle one responded.

'Er, no, I don't think we do. To be honest, I didn't think we had to.'

'Well, yes, I really think you do. We only allow active account holders to make withdrawals. Have any of you had an account with us before?'

'Er…' the middle bank robber looked at his chums again, who were already staring at him, shaking their heads and looking a little disheartened. 'No… I don't think any of us have.' But then he had an idea, and continued with a more upbeat tone of voice. 'My Mum might have though. Would that help?'

'Well, maybe, yes, but she'd have to come here in person, to make the withdrawal.'

Becky couldn't quite believe what she was hearing, but as her mouth was still stuffed full of sandwich, she was forced to stand there and keep out of it, which she was finding rather difficult.

The shorter bank robber had another idea.

'What if we were to open accounts now? Would that help?'

'Well, yes, I suppose so, but we'd need to see some sort of identification, and a proof of address; a driving licence or something.'

Checking his coat, the shorter one said, 'I don't have a driver's license but I think my Mum's sewn my name on my coat somewhere; would that count?'

'Does it include a photograph?' asked Brian.

'No, I don't think so.'

'Then no, sorry, sir, we really need something with a photograph, like a passport perhaps.'

The three men conferred again, but none of them had anything like that.

'OK, I'll call my Mum and see if she does have an account here. Hold on,' and with that the shorter one, still in the middle, reached inside his jeans pocket and pulled out his smartphone.

Seeing him do so reminded the others that they hadn't checked their emails since before they walked in, so they also pulled their phones out. But it was then that the shorter one realised that he was going to need both hands to dial the number and looked around for someone to hold his gun. However, with all three of them now with a smartphone in one hand, and a gun in the other, his eyes eventually fell on Becky, who was cramming the last of her sandwich into her mouth.

'I don't suppose you could hold this for me?' he asked.

Becky snorted with disbelief, nearly choking in the process, but as she was still completely unable to talk, she shoved the empty sandwich packet back into her bag and, with both hands now free, helped the man out.

Now the shorter bank robber was able to dial, and after a slight delay, began a whole different conversation.

'Hello Mum, it's Mark! How are you? Yes, fine thanks. I'm at the bank. No, not yet, I'll do it later. Listen Mum, who do you bank with? Is it the Instathon or Nationwide? Oh, OK, no, don't worry, no problem. I was just curious, that's all. Yes. Thanks, Mum. I'll be back in time for tea. See you then!'

He ended the call and looked back at the Bank Manager.

'No, sorry. She's with Nationwide.'

Having finally swallowed the last of her sandwich,

Becky couldn't contain herself any longer.

'Seriously?' she asked, staring at them. 'Is this some sort of a joke?'

All three of them looked at her, confused.

'Do you boys have any idea what you're doing? For Christ's sake, you don't need an account if you're robbing a bank! I think the idea is that if you've got guns, you just point them at people and they give you money.'

The masked men all stared at her as if she was the one with three heads.

Becky rolled her eyes and turned to the Bank Manager, levelling the gun at him without realising.

'Brian, can you please go and get all the money from the safe and bring it out here, so we can get on with our day?'

'Er, yes of course, Becky,' he said, and edged his way backwards with his eyes fixed on the shotgun that was now pointing straight at his groin.

'Oh, and Brian, whilst you're there, prop that fire extinguisher up against the door. That will help keep it open.'

'Yes... of course, Becky. Good idea!' and he brought his hands down to un-hook the nearby fire extinguisher and place it on the floor against the now open door. Then he walked slowly past the two remaining cashiers and disappeared out the back.

'Tanya, Lisa, go help him will you? He's not exactly quick at the best of times. Oh, and get Trisha to help too. She's probably still crying in the toilet somewhere.'

Suddenly there was a sucking sound from behind Becky and out of the corner of her eye she saw an old woman, attempting to open the bank's door. Becky turned and said, 'I'm really sorry, madam, but the bank's closed.'

The old lady continued pulling at the door with all her strength, and when she'd managed to open it halfway, poked her head in and said, 'I'm sorry dear, what did you say?'

'THE BANK'S CLOSED, SORRY. YOU'LL HAVE TO COME BACK LATER.'

'Oh, alright my dear, I'll come back later then. So, shall I come back later?'

'YES PLEASE, THANK YOU.'

The old lady smiled, nodded and allowed the door to shove her back into the high street.

Becky spun back around and spoke directly to the three bank robbers.

'Right, one of you will need to cover the door,' and she pointed her gun at the guy nearest who nodded obediently and went to make sure nobody else tried to get in.

'Another of you needs to go through to the back and get the security cameras turned off and remove the footage. And the other needs to turn off the alarm before Brian remembers to set it off. It's around the back, near the fuse box. Someone will show you.'

Both men nodded and made their way to the back office.

'And tell them to hurry up with the money, we haven't got all bloody day!'

Feeling more in control of her life again, Becky felt much better.

Behind her a love-struck young couple attempted to enter the bank, but the masked man who now guarded the entrance simply tapped his shotgun on the glass and said in a loud, ominous voice, 'SORRY, WE'RE CLOSED!'

Somewhat alarmed by Instathon's high level of security, the couple turned around and headed back into the high street to try NatWest instead.

Just then, Brian and the three cashiers came out from the back carrying four heavy grey sacks, stuffed full of cash, and waddled their way past the glass panels and out through the main security door, now jammed open with the fire extinguisher. They were all breathing hard and visibly sagging with each step. When they finally reached the middle of the foyer they dropped their sacks before leaning over on their knees, gasping for breath.

As the two remaining bank robbers followed them out, Becky asked, 'Did you disable the alarms?'

Smiling through their ski masks, they nodded.

'And the camera recordings?'

They each held up a compact disc.

'Good job. Now, get your masks off and grab a bag.'

Then to Brian she said, 'I'm just going to pop out to give them a hand with the money, I'll be back in about ten minutes, is that OK?'

'Oh, well, er, yes, I suppose so Becky, and er…well, thank you for all your help but please, don't be too long.'

And with that, Becky and the three robbers picked up a sack each and she led the way out into the natural light of Bath's bustling High Street.

As soon as they were outside, and the door had closed itself, Becky asked, 'Right, where's your car?'

'Oh, we don't have a car.'

Becky stopped dead in her tracks, and the others bunched up behind her, forcing eager shoppers to push and shove their way past. She turned around to face them.

'I'm sorry, for a second there I thought you said that you didn't have a car.'

'Yes, that's right, we don't.'

'So exactly how did you expect to get away?' she asked with insurmountable curiosity.

'Well, we only live up there.'

It was the shorter of the robbers talking again, and he pointed at some place which seemed to be miles away. 'We thought we'd just walk home.'

Becky looked over to where the man was pointing.

It *was* miles away!

'Right, follow me then, my car's just around the corner. I'll give you a lift, half way at least.'

So they all followed after her as she marched off with a massive sack stuffed full of cash under one arm, and a sawn-off shotgun under the other. With the rather insistent sound of the bank's alarm now chasing them, they crossed the road opposite The Corridor, and followed the one-way system around to where Becky had parked, just past the art gallery on the right.

CHAPTER III
QUEN TE IPSUM FACIS?
Just who the hell do you think you are?

IT WAS A BRIGHT, sparkling summer's day in the historic City of Bath and Inspector Capstan was being given no time to enjoy it. At that moment he was being hurtled up Pierrepont Street towards the roundabout at the end, in a blur of blue flashing lights, screaming sirens, bewildered tourists and scattering cyclists.

Not only was he being given no time to enjoy the glorious weather, but he wasn't being given much of a chance to take in the sights either. The elegant Parade Gardens passed by in a flash of green on his right and, half a second later, Bath Abbey flickered past to his left, and he really wanted to see that as well. He'd only had a chance to look at it once before, and that was when he'd popped up there with his wife and children for the job interview; after all, this was only his very first week with Bath City Police, having just moved up from Kingston-on-Thames in Surrey.

Only the month before he'd managed to complete his Fast Track Graduate Police Training Programme, the one that had catapulted him from "Grubby Graduate" to "Shiny New" Police Inspector in just three short years. And by the time he'd finished his training, he'd been living in Kingston for well over six years, and had grown tired of the place. It was there that he'd picked up his degree in Social Media, it was there that he'd done something similar with the girl who was now his wife, and it was there that she'd popped out their two children. He'd subsequently been looking for a change of scenery and, more importantly, somewhere where he could afford to buy a house. The prices in Surrey were way beyond his salary range, even at Police Inspector level.

So, it was with some good fortune that the job had come up in Bath, and, although not the adrenaline-fuelled location that he had hoped to find, he could at least afford to buy a small semi on the outskirts of town.

Having been alerted about the bank robbery only a few minutes earlier, local boy Sergeant Dewbush was now accelerating him towards the scene of the crime, about half a mile up the road from the police station; and although Capstan couldn't help but be a little apprehensive, as this was his first major callout since arriving, he'd still liked to have had the chance to enjoy the sparkliness of the day, and maybe to have stared up at Bath Abbey's resplendent gothic architecture. But it was not to be, because no sooner had he realised that the flash of grey over to his left was in fact the Abbey, the car had screeched to a halt outside the Instathon Bank, just up from Cheap Street.

As soon as the car stopped, and Capstan was able to remove his face from the passenger side window, he checked to make sure that they'd managed to miss the bright red open-topped tour bus that he'd seen trying to steer clear of them, without losing too many passengers from its top deck. Relieved to see that they'd achieved the impossible, he glanced back through the car's rear window to make sure they hadn't hit anything, or anyone, else. Seeing no corpses scattered in their wake, he reached over to silence the ear-bleeding noise of the sirens. Only then did he consider it safe to open the door.

One of the first lessons he'd learnt during his police training was never to open a police car door until its sirens had been turned off. He had done this once, by mistake, and had been lucky to escape with only a temporary loss of hearing. Others he'd known hadn't faired so well, suffering permanent ear damage as a result. But with the sirens now silent, both he and Dewbush stepped out of the car.

Directly ahead of them stood the bank, and someone who seemed unable to stop fidgeting.

Brian had made his way there just as soon as he'd been able to set the alarm off. As he'd listened to the distant siren speed its way ever closer, he had tried to decide what his overall demeanour should be: that of a concerned Bank Manager who'd been fleeced of every penny, or a happy-go-lucky one who might be about to pick up some new customers from the local police community. But having now had time to consider the matter, and having seen the way this unmarked police car had to do a hand-brake turn in order to miss Bath's famous red open-topped tour bus, which still had several tourists hanging from the top, he now watched these two men walk towards him with their ominous gait and decided that it was probably best to stick with "concerned Bank Manager who'd just been fleeced of every penny."

'Hello, you must be the police,' he said and pushed

his right hand out for a warm, welcoming handshake.

Both Capstan and Dewbush looked down at the offered hand and tried to decide what action they should take. It was against police policy to shake hands in the line of duty. It was just too dangerous. So they both stared down at it, and then up again at the man, and kept doing that until such time as the man decided that he'd made a mistake, and withdrew the unwanted hand, only to start wringing it out with the other one.

With the Case of the Proffered Hand now solved, Capstan was able to continue with his formal introduction.

'Yes, that's right. I'm Inspector Capstan and this is Sergeant Dewbush.'

At this stage Capstan would normally pull out his formal identification, but he really couldn't be bothered. Dewbush couldn't either, but he did take out his little black notebook and pen.

'And you are?' Capstan asked.

Dewbush poised himself, ready to write the name down.

'Oh, sorry, my name's Brian Haverlington, I'm the Bank Manager here. I'm certainly very pleased you've come; you see, it would appear that we've been robbed!'

'Yes, we know that, Mr Haverlington, that's why we're here,' said Capstan, happy to make this little man, who was clearly a bit dim, feel even more stupid than he must do whenever he happened to look in a mirror. There was something about him, which Capstan couldn't quite put his finger on, but which normally meant that the person was hiding some guilty secret about an as yet undiscovered crime, so Capstan decided to use his very best, and most official, Policeman's Smile, the one he'd been taught to use that said, '*We know you've done something highly illegal at some point in your life, we just haven't found out about it yet!*' simply to see what effect it would have.

'Yes, of course,' said Brian, who'd started to sweat. 'Won't you please come in?'

Brian pulled open the heavy glass door and ushered them both inside.

On entering, Capstan and Dewbush had a quick look around. In front of the reception desk was a group of people who they assumed to be the bank's customers, all taking various "selfies" of themselves and posting them up on Facebook, or some other Social Media site, probably along with a comment about how they'd been involved in an exciting armed robbery. Those who hadn't quite made the quantum leap into Social Media still stood around taking "selfies", but instead of posting them up somewhere, were phoning up everyone they knew, one at a time. And as this mini photo-phone fest took place, two of the cashiers were busy fetching cups of tea and coffee whilst the rather large one busied herself pulling chairs out from the back for everyone to sit on.

Meanwhile, the bank's Line Manager was standing just inside the main entrance, turning away any arriving customers by asking them to come back tomorrow, as they'd had to close early for the day because they'd just been robbed by a gang of dangerous criminals who'd worn black ski-masks and were armed to the teeth with massive shotguns. Of course, she wasn't supposed to be telling anyone at all, as it wasn't the sort of PR that Instathon liked to have bandied about too much, but it was far too exciting for her to keep to herself.

Dewbush's phone rang, and he went off to take the call.

Seeing that he was now faced with only one policeman, instead of two, Brian felt less intimidated and more able to talk.

'We asked all the customers to stay behind until you arrived, in case you needed to ask them any questions.'

'Thank you, yes.' said Capstan. 'If you could just have someone take down their names, addresses and phone numbers, they can go home. We'll contact them later, if necessary.'

Brian nodded and slunk off to give the cashier girls their new instructions.

Dewbush returned.

'Forensics will be here any minute, Sir.'

'Good, but I can't imagine they'll have much luck. Looks like the place has been trampled over by half the City!'

Brian returned, still sweating and wringing his hands, and with all three of them back together again, Capstan thought he'd push on with the investigation.

'So Mr, er…'

'Oh, Haverlington, Brian Haverlington.'

'So, Mr Haverlington, in your own words, can you tell me exactly what happened?'

'Well, yes. I can try at least. I was in the back office, checking over the projected forecast for the month, when Patricia came in from the front. She was in a terrible state, all teary-eyed and blubbering about how the place was being robbed and how one of them had called her fat.' Brian looked over his shoulder and leaned in. 'She's very sensitive about her weight, you see. She's also prone to exaggerating certain things, like how many boyfriends she has. None of us think she has any at all, but she's always boasting about them and exactly what she's done with them all.' He glanced back over his shoulder again, to make sure he hadn't been overheard, and then continued. 'Anyway, I popped my head out from the back and that's when I saw that she was telling the truth - for a change,' he added in a meaningful whisper. 'So I came out to see what they wanted.'

Brian stopped talking, so Capstan felt it necessary to give him a little prompt.

'And what exactly did they want?'

'Oh, they wanted all the money.'

Capstan was unsure as to why he'd asked that, but Brian had stopped talking again so he had to ask him something else.

'Yes, well, I suppose they did. And what happened next?'

'I asked if they had an account with us. It's the bank's policy to only allow active account holders to make cash withdrawals, but none of them did.'

'Right,' said Capstan, unsure what to say to that, but fortunately Brian continued.

'Then they asked if they could open an account, but only one of them had any form of identification, which was his name, sown on the inside of his coat; only his name, mind, not a photograph or anything, so we couldn't accept it.'

'OK,' said Capstan, becoming increasingly puzzled as to how this could have any bearing on the case.

'But then one of them remembered that his mother

might have an account with us, so he phoned her up to ask her.'

He was now beginning to hope that the Bank Manager would stop talking, as none of this was making any sense, but he clearly hadn't finished, so he decided to prompt him once more, hoping that the answer to his next question may indeed have some relevance.

'And did the suspect's Mother have an account here?'

'Regrettably not. She's with Nationwide.'

Failing to see how any of this could have anything to do with anything at all, Capstan was just considering the idea of arresting the man for wasting police time when he started talking again, all on his own.

'And that was when Becky pointed her gun at me and asked me to get the money. So I went through to the safe at the back, placed all the unmarked bills into four large, grey postal bags, and brought them out here, to the front. Then all four of them left with the money, at which point I raised the alarm.'

By now even Dewbush had stopped writing and had joined Capstan as they both stared uncomprehendingly at this short, bald man who was making no sense whatsoever. But at least he'd reached the end of his rather bizarre account of the robbery and now just stood there, wringing his hands, and sweating.

Dewbush looked back at his notes and asked, 'I'm sorry, I thought you said there were three of them?'

'Yes, that's right, three men wearing black masks with holes cut out for their eyes, nose and mouth.'

'But you said that four people left with the money.'

'Yes. That was Becky.'
'What was Becky?'
'The fourth one.'
'So there were four then?'
'No, only three. Becky was just giving them a hand.'
'Giving them a hand with what?'
'With the money.'

Dewbush was none the wiser, and looked over to Capstan for help, but he was equally clueless.

Thinking that it was probably his turn to ask some more questions, in the vague hope that one of them might provide a meaningful answer, Capstan asked, 'So, just exactly who is this Becky person then?'

'Becky, er… Becky Phillips. She works here. Well, in the afternoons anyway, Monday to Friday. She's what we call a Part-Time Employee.'

'And where is she now?'

'As I said, she left with the bank robbers,' continued Brian, who'd briefly stopped wringing his hands to look down at his watch. 'Actually, she should be back any minute now,' and he glanced around the bank to see if she'd come in without him noticing. 'Anyway, she was helping them carry the money out. There was rather a lot of it, and they had their guns as well.'

Dewbush had managed to check back through his notes to find the part he was looking for.

'But you said that it was Becky who pointed the gun at you and told you to get the money?'

'Yes, that's right.'

'But… if she worked for you, why did she have a gun?'

'Oh, I think it was one of the robber's.'

'So, she was one of them then?'

'Oh no, I don't think so.'

'But you said that it was her who pointed the gun at you, and then told you to get the money.'

'Well, yes, as I said, I think she was just trying to be helpful. They seemed to be struggling a bit and Becky's always been very good with the customers.'

Capstan jumped in.

'Yes, but Mr Haverlington, they weren't customers though, were they? They were heavily armed criminals!'

'Well, that's as maybe, but we'd only just established that they didn't have an account with us, and they did seem awfully keen to open one. I think Becky was just being her normal helpful self.'

'By pointing a gun at you and asking you to get all the money?'

'Well, no - but yes.'

'And then by leaving, with the men, and the money?'

'Er, well, sort of, yes,' repeated Brian, looking back at his watch.

From Capstan's point of view it now seemed fairly obvious that this was an inside job, and that it was this Becky Phillips who was behind the whole thing, and with that in mind he ploughed on.

'So, you're telling me that three masked men forced their way into the bank and, having secured the premises, gave this Becky girl one of their guns which she proceeded to point at you before ordering you to get all the money, which you did. Then all four of them left, with the money. Is that correct?'

When put like that it did seem rather odd, and

Brian was now forced to think back, trying to remember if Becky had indeed been one of the robbers. But having mentally revisited the scene, he recalled that she hadn't been wearing a mask and had just been standing there, eating a sandwich, and so it really didn't seem likely.

'I'm probably not explaining myself very well. Becky was standing about where you are now, having her lunch, when one of the bank robbers asked her to hold his gun for him so that he could phone his mother. That was when she asked me if I could pop to the safe to get the money. I'm sure she had nothing more to do with it than that.'

'So why did you get the money if it was only this Becky girl asking for it?' questioned Capstan, still convinced that the girl must have been behind the whole thing.

'Oh, they'd asked me before then, I just hadn't had a chance to clarify if they had an account with us.'

'So, when Becky asked you, then it was OK?'

'Well yes, she works here; that automatically entitles her to an account.'

'Am I correct in understanding that anyone who has an account with the Instathon Bank can walk in here, at any time, and take out just as much money as they want, whenever they like?'

'Well no, obviously not, but having an account does at least allow us to clarify how much money they can take out.'

Capstan was getting nowhere again and decided to try a different tack.

'Do you have any prior criminal convictions, Mr. Haverlington?'

Brian suddenly went very pale, stopped wringing his hands and started to sweat profusely.

'Well, I, er, um, I really, no, I mean, I'm not sure what that has to do with anything?'

Jackpot! thought Capstan, and a big, broad smile spread over his face.

'So, just exactly how long have you and Becky been planning this whole thing for then?'

Brian's heart jumped inside his chest and his knees buckled underneath him. His bottom lip began to wobble and tears welled up in his eyes. The mere thought of being sent to prison was having an alarming effect on his entire body. His heart pounded hard in his throat and he was feeling increasingly sick. He'd also become frozen to the spot and was struggling to maintain control of his bowels. As he started to tremble uncontrollably, he found himself having to use all his will-power not to start sobbing, right there in the middle of his own bank. And with all this going on inside his body, his mind raced around, desperately trying to remember if he had planned the whole thing after all, and had simply forgotten about it. But no, it just wasn't possible; he knew he couldn't be capable of such a premeditated criminal act, and having firmly established that fact, he was able to regain control of himself, enough to speak at least.

'No, there's clearly been some... terrible misunderstanding. I'm sure that if you could only speak to Becky, she'd be able to explain the whole thing to you.'

At that moment, Becky walked in.

'Explain what exactly, Brian?'

With an overwhelming sense of joy, Brian gazed up

at Becky half crying, half dancing, and skipped over to envelop her in a warm, loving embrace, as if she were his long-lost daughter whom he hadn't seen since she was five. Fortunately, just before he reached her, he remembered his position and that he'd already been cautioned by the police about inappropriately touching female members of staff, so he pulled out some tissues from his pocket, dried his eyes and said, as unemotionally as possible, 'Ah, there you are Becky, welcome back! I was just telling these two nice young policemen about the three bank robbers, and how they managed to get away with all our money.'

'So you're Becky?' asked Capstan, swinging around to direct all his attention at this extremely attractive young woman.

Becky could see that Brian was very unhappy, and as he'd been fine when she'd left, it stood to reason that it must have been one of these two who'd managed to upset him so much.

'Yes, that's right,' she answered, 'and just who the hell are you?' She levelled her gaze at both Capstan and Dewbush whilst rolling her sleeves up, mentally preparing for a fist fight.

Seeing her intentions, they both felt it necessary to show her their police identification.

'I'm Police Inspector Capstan and this is Sergeant Dewbush. We're here about the robbery.'

'Well, I didn't think you were here for a loan!'

Becky smiled to herself, realising that she'd just been unusually funny.

'Yes, quite,' said Capstan, feeling a little hurt at what he felt was an unnecessary joke at his expense. 'I understand you work here. Is that correct?'

'Yes, that is correct.'

'And may I ask where you've been?'

'Yes, of course!'

Then she just stood there, put both hands on her hips and shook out her dark brown hair somewhat provocatively.

After a few moments Capstan decided to ask his question again, but this time with a little less ambiguity.

'So, Becky, where have you been?'

'I was helping the bank robbers with the money. I'm surprised Brian didn't tell you.'

'Well, yes, Brian, I mean Mr Haverlington has been explaining it to us,' and he glanced over at Dewbush before adding, 'sort of, but I was hoping you could tell us the story from your perspective.'

'Sure, no problem. These three guys walked in here about, what, half an hour ago, wearing black ski-masks and carrying sawn-off shot guns, and they took all our money.'

'Yes, thank you. But Mr Haverlington said that you had a gun as well?'

'Yes, that's right.'

Capstan was surprised she hadn't tried to deny this.

'And what, may I ask, where you doing with the gun?'

'I was holding it.'

'Yes, but with what intention?'

'So that one of the bank robbers could call his mum.'

Not allowing himself to be taken down the whole, "calling his mum to see if she had an account" path again, he brought the conversation back to where he wanted it to be.

'But we understand you pointed the gun at Mr. Haverlington and then told him to get all the money. Is that correct?'

'Not really, but go on,' and she folded her arms and pouted at him.

Capstan was beginning to find himself becoming extremely attracted to this dangerous young woman, and this feeling of general arousal really wasn't helping with his line of enquiry. And as he became increasingly aware of just how attractive she was, he found himself starting to blush and had to clear his throat before attempting to carry on.

'And that's when you left with the bank robbers and all the money. Is that correct?'

'Yes, that's right. You know, you really are very good at this,' she said, and smiled seductively at him. Becky was enjoying herself and she had no idea why.

Reaching up to pull his collar away from the prickly heat that he could feel growing around his neck, he continued, 'And now you're back here, again,' knowing that it was a really stupid thing to say, and hating himself for saying it.

'That's right, I'm back, here, again,' she said, and replaced her hands on her hips and pushed her breasts out.

Meanwhile Dewbush looked up from his notes to Capstan, then to the girl, and back to Capstan again, trying to work out exactly where his boss was going with this rather peculiar line of questioning.

Capstan shook his head in an effort to regain his focus, and in a bid to stop himself from going red he thought up another question.

'So, Miss Philips, where exactly did you go, when

you left the bank?'

'Oh, I gave them a lift. None of them had a car, you see, and they all lived miles away. So as I was parked just around the corner I thought I could give them a ride home, well, half-way at least. I didn't want to be too long, as I'd already told Brian that I'd be back in a few minutes.'

Having now had the chance to examine this girl's anatomy as she postured herself in front of him, he began to feel aroused all over again, and decided that he'd probably be better off just making sure that they had everyone's details before retreating back to his office to consider the evidence, with a cool head and a hot coffee, and without wanting to become intimate with one of the key suspects every time he happened to look at her. He was married, after all, and really didn't think it sensible to begin an affair during the very first week of starting his new job.

'OK, that will do for now,' he said to the room as a whole. 'Thank you all for being so patient.'

Dewbush piped up.

'How about the camera footage, Sir?'

'Oh yes, thank you, Dewbush. Mr Haverlington, can you please ask someone to bring out the CCTV footage for the day.'

'Oh, er, sorry, but they took that with them as well.'

'So they did have some idea as to what they were doing then?' Capstan asked, with grave suspicion, and keen to highlight the fact that maybe they didn't need quite as much help as had previously been insinuated.

'Actually, it was my idea,' Becky called out. 'I thought it would be nice for them to have the footage, as a little memento. I thought they might like to upload it to YouTube, for their friends to see.'

That really was too much for Capstan. As attractive as she was, she was clearly guilty as hell, so he started up again with renewed resolve.

'So, you're trying to tell me that you just happened to be here at exactly the same time as the bank robbers, that you had a gun, that you pointed that gun at Mr Haverlington, that you told him to get all the money from the safe, that you left with the money, and the bank robbers, that you gave them all a lift home - sorry, half-way home, and then, before they left, you made sure that they'd taken the video evidence; and after doing all that, you still deny having had any criminal involvement?'

Capstan had no idea what he'd just let loose. She headed straight for him and started to unleash a verbal assault that would have brought the bravest man to his knees.

'Just who the hell do you think you are, coming into our bank, pushing your weight around as if you own the place, upsetting Brian for no good reason and then having the gall to accuse me, ME, of armed robbery? You do understand that I work here, don't you? We all work here, for Christ sake! Do you work here? Do you? You probably don't even live here! And now you're insinuating that I woke up this morning and decided to join a gang of armed robbers, so that I could rob the very bank at which I work? Are you a complete moron or is it just that you look like one? I've heard all policemen are a bit dim, but you really are taking it to a whole new level! Do I look like a bank robber? Am I wearing a mask? Do I have a gun? I know I've said this before but I WORK HERE,

FOR CHRIST'S SAKE!'

Capstan was totally out of his depth. He was also experiencing a range of conflicting emotions that he was struggling to contend with. The sensitive side of him wanted to run off and hide in a cupboard somewhere, his more masculine side thought he really should have a go at arresting her on suspicion of armed robbery, and his hormonal side wanted to ask for her phone number. And whilst these conflicting emotions all jockeyed for position inside his head, the only response he could come up with was, 'Well no, of course we're not suggesting that you robbed the place, it's just that it does seem a little odd that you were... possibly in possession of a gun which you may have pointed at Mr... er, Brian, and then you happened to leave with the money at the same time as all the other bank robbers did.'

All the while he'd been edging himself away from this tornado of raw feminine fury, but he was beginning to run out of room. And when her face was just inches away from his, she held her ground and, using one of her long, slender fingers, prodded at his chest saying, 'Now listen, Cat Spam or whatever your name is, we have a strict policy here at the Instathon Bank that states, in no uncertain terms, that the customer is always right. Isn't that so, Brian?'

'Yes, quite right, Becky, quite right!'

Brian was absolutely thrilled to be watching the police being torn to pieces like this, and by his favourite employee as well!

Capstan retaliated.

'But they weren't really customers though, were they? They were armed bank robbers!'

Becky backed off and returned to her former stance.

'Look, as far as the Instathon is concerned, anyone who enters through those doors is either a customer or a potential customer, and he or she should be treated as such at all times. I was simply being as considerate as possible, and in exactly the way I've been taught during our various customer training days.'

'Quite right, Becky, quite right!' said Brian again, wanting to jump, dance and clap, but managing to restrain himself.

Capstan capitulated. Just outside he could hear a van's side door being slid closed, which he assumed must be Forensics, and thought it best to retreat back to his office and reflect on the matter from there.

'Well, thank you all very much for being so... cooperative. I won't take up any more of your time,' and with that he turned to make his way outside with a strange mixture of relief, disappointment and intense sexual frustration.

But as he began to head out, Dewbush grabbed his arm.

'Sir, just to warn you, the press are waiting for you outside!'

He stopped dead in his tracks and looked back at Dewbush with sheer desperation.

'Really?' he asked, automatically straightening his tie. He'd completely forgotten about the press and that dealing with them was now part of his job. 'Can't I speak to them later?'

'I'm sorry, Sir, but this is quite a major incident for Bath, and I'm sure they're going to want some sort of a statement from you.'

'Christ!'

He flattened his hair, straightened his tie and did up the middle button of his suit before turning to Dewbush to ask, 'Do I look all right?' somewhat self-consciously.

Dewbush suppressed a smirk and looked him straight in the eye and said, in the only way one heterosexual policeman could ever say to another without appearing to be completely gay, 'You look fine, Sir.'

Not convinced, Capstan stared out through the bank's glass door at the awaiting press, took another deep breath and marched forward, out onto High Street, with Dewbush trailing behind.

CHAPTER IV
QUAERITUR TEMPORE
Question time

AS SOON as he'd stepped into the daylight, a barrage of flash-photography erupted causing him to squint and raise a hand to protect his eyes from retinal damage before treading more carefully into the melee.

Sensing this was their quarry, the press started to fire out questions, all at the same time. Pitching his voice so that he could be heard, he introduced himself.

'Hello everyone, my name's Police Inspector Capstan. I understand you have some...'

A tiny blond girl at the front, who'd been squirming with her hand in the air like a schoolgirl desperate to go to the toilet, shouted out, 'Liz Herbert, Daily Bath. Was the bank robbed?'

'Yes, unfortunately the bank has been robbed,' he replied, hoping that all the questions would be that easy.

'Did they have guns?'

'Again, yes, they were all heavily armed.'

'Was anyone killed?'

'Fortunately nobody was killed, no!'

'Was anyone injured?'

'Nobody was injured either.'

'Was anyone hurt in any way?'

'Er, no, nobody's been hurt in any way, as far as I know.'

'So someone may have been hurt, you just don't know about it yet?'

'Well, yes, I suppose it's possible, but if they have been then I'm sure it's nothing serious.'

'Do you know exactly how they were hurt? Were they shot? Can we speak to them?'

'Again, no, I really don't think anyone has been hurt at all, and even if they have, now's probably not the best time to talk to them.'

'So, someone was shot then?'

Capstan wasn't prepared for this. They hadn't covered speaking to the press during his Police training.

'No, nobody was shot!'

'Were there any shots fired?'

'No, I don't believe there were.'

'Might there have been shots fired that you don't know about yet?'

'Well, again, yes, I suppose there could have been shots fired, but if there were, then nobody was hurt by them.'

'Was any money stolen?'

'Yes, I'm afraid that the suspects were able to escape with a large sum.'

'How much?'

He'd forgotten to ask that one himself.

'At this stage we're not sure exactly, but we believe it to be a significant amount.'

'Did they get away?'

Capstan was already flagging.

'Yes, unfortunately they did seem to have been able

to effect an escape.'

'Do you know how?'

He was very tempted to answer that truthfully, but having seen the result even an indirect accusation had on Becky, he thought better of it.

'I believe they made their escape by car.'

'Do you know who they are?'

Apparently, if they'd all left their clothes behind, then maybe he would.

'No, unfortunately, we've yet to establish their identities.'

'How many were there?'

Another awkward question and he looked back over his shoulder to Dewbush for clarification, but Dewbush just stared back at him and shrugged, not willing to commit himself. Capstan wasn't too keen either, so he tried to be as vague as possible, without appearing to be completely inept.

'At least three?' he answered, unable to prevent it from sounding like a question.

There was a slight pause during which he hoped nobody was going to pin him down for a more accurate answer.

'Were there any witnesses?'

With some relief to be moving on, Capstan replied, 'Yes, we've still to take formal statements from the bank's staff and all the customers who happened to be caught up in the crime.'

'Where did the bank robbers go when they left?'

He made a mental note to ask Becky that one, but for now he just answered, 'We're not sure at present, but we'll be making further enquiries.'

'How long before you make an arrest?'

'This is a very serious crime and we'll be doing all that we can to ascertain exactly who is responsible, just as quickly as possible.'

'Are you expecting to recover the money?'

'It is our intention to, yes.'

Up until now the battery of questions had been coming from the same blond reporter who at last looked like she'd been to the toilet and felt much better for it.

Probably feeling either left out or that they should be doing something more than just standing there with someone else making up all the questions, some of the other reporters interjected their own.

'Can we speak to some of the staff?' one called out.

'Can we speak to some of the customers?' another cried.

'Did they have masks on?'

'Are they dangerous?'

'What type of guns did they have?'

'What were they wearing?'

'Are they from Bath?'

'What's their star sign?'

'What's your star sign?'

'Do you have a dog?'

'What colour is it?'

'What's its name?'

As much fun as it was watching his boss being mangled by the press, Dewbush thought he'd better come to his rescue.

'That will be all for now,' he said. 'Thank you for your questions,' and grabbed Capstan's arm, forcibly pushing him through the throng of press towards their car.

Curious to know where they were going, the paparazzi followed after them and continued with their strange, canine-related interrogation.

'What sort of dog is it?'

'Does it like Baxters or Pedigree Chum?'

'Do you have two dogs or one?'

'Who takes it for a walk?'

They both clambered into the car and slammed the doors closed.

'Jesus Christ!' exclaimed Capstan. 'What's with all the bloody dog questions?'

'Oh, it was Bath's Annual Dog Show last weekend. I don't think they've forgotten about it yet.'

'No, clearly! But why do they think I've got a dog?'

'I've no idea, Sir.'

Dewbush started the engine and, ignoring the frenzied mob who had now started to bash on the glass next to his head, asked, 'Do you have a dog, Sir?'

'Of course I don't have a bloody dog! I've got a wife and two kids! Why on earth would I want a dog?'

The press-pack split and attempted a two-pronged attack, and with Capstan now avoiding eye contact with those reporters banging against his window, Dewbush said, 'Tell you what, Sir, I'll put the sirens on, that will clear them.'

With the sirens blaring, the blue lights spinning and the paparazzi scattering with their hands flattened against their ears and their cameras dangling around their necks, Dewbush slipped the car into first, put his foot down hard on the accelerator and released the clutch to leave the smell of burning rubber and an accompanying cloud of smoke to mask their rather dramatic departure.

Heading back down Pierpont Street in relative silence, Dewbush thought he'd make conversation.

'So, what did you think of all that then, Sir?'

'I think Bath's completely obsessed with dogs, that's what I think!'

'I meant about the case, Sir. The bank robbery.'

'Oh that's easy. That Becky girl is clearly up to her neck in it. First thing tomorrow I'll bring her in for questioning.'

Capstan's mobile started to ring and he dug his hand into his inside breast pocket to dig it out. 'If nothing else,' he continued, 'we need to find out where she dropped off her little "friends". I wouldn't be surprised if she gave them a lift all the way home and that she knows exactly where they're hiding out.'

He pressed the green answer button.

'Hello, Capstan here!'

There was a long pause as he listened to the caller.

'Last night?'

Another pause.

'Are they sure?'

Silence again.

'Can't someone else deal with it?'

The car continued heading down towards the station.

'OK, fine, we'll head over there now. Yes, thanks, bye.'

Capstan pressed the red button and slipped the phone back inside his suit as he asked, 'Have you heard of a place called the Roman Basin Museum?'

'Yes, of course, Sir. It's right next door to the Roman Baths. Do you fancy a bit of sight-seeing?'

'No, you bloody idiot! They were broken into last

night.'

'Really?'

'Yes, really! They've found a window that's been forced and a few items are missing. We'd better head over.'

'Righty-ho.' Without even glancing into his rear-view mirror, Dewbush did another hand-break turn, slap-bang in the middle of the road, spinning the car around and accelerating it back up the way they'd just come, sirens blazing, lights still spinning.

CHAPTER V
AQUAE SULIS
The Roman Baths

THE CITY of Bath's historic Basin Museum rests alongside its big brother, the slightly better known, and far more popular, Roman Baths. They're both World Heritage Sites, they're both fed by the same natural springs, they're both accessible from York Street and they've both enjoyed an intense rivalry ever since the Saxons kicked the Romans out in 577 AD.

The dispute started shortly afterwards. The Roman name of Aquae Sulis was ditched, of course - far too pompous and arrogant - but removing the name did leave them needing another. They knew it had to be something that related to the unique hot spring waters, and a number of alternatives were suggested, which included Wash, Clothes, Soap, Dish, Tap and Water. They even came up with an interesting word combination of Tap Water, but after much debate the choice finally came down to two; Bath or Basin.

Looking back at recorded historical documentation, it's clear that the Saxons had two distinct methods of self-cleansing, "bathing", which took place in an outdoors environment, or "basining" which took place indoors. The outside "Bathers" supported the name Bath, as they felt it represented what they believed to be the correct way to clean the body; free, natural and open. The "Basiners", however, were intent on the settlement being called Basin, as they felt this represented their more civilised approach.

After much toing, froing and wife swapping, a fierce battle broke out between the two factions leaving the Basiners defeated and the Bathers victorious. So the rather unusual name of Bath was adopted, but for hundreds of years the same bitter rivalry grumbled on between the two factions, until, by the time the late 20th Century had arrived, the dispute had been distilled down to whether or not one preferred the Roman Baths or the Roman Basins.

Unlike its more famous brother, the Roman Basins feature a number of indoor swimming pool-type structures. There are six in total, three on one side and three on the other, each housed within its own separate chamber and all linked by a single corridor.

The basins were all built with the exact same dimensions of length, width and depth; 10 x 6 x 3 Roman cubitus or 14.4 x 8.6 x 4.2 feet, and identical in size, they were also identical in design, all having the same ornately carved stone steps leading down to their bases. It's considered that the chamber walls themselves originally displayed the most beautifully coloured frescos imaginable, depicting detailed scenes of everyday life in Roman Britain. Unfortunately only two survived, and these became the museum's main attraction, excluding the Basins themselves of course.

As international tourism and sight-seeing became more attainable during the 1960's and 70's, it became evident that the Roman Baths were much more popular. This was when the Basin's Curators began to import large numbers of ancient artefacts all the way from Rome, to help attract a few more tourists. Such rare pieces included a good number of statues, a few earthenware pots and a massive collection of army equipment including shields, swords, daggers, armour and throwing spears, most of which had been so well looked after that it was difficult to distinguish them from the shiny new ones manufactured by film studios the world over. But with space limited, and not being able to afford the rent for local storage facilities, the curators had, over time, piled them all up in two of the basins at the farthest end of the corridor, which allowed them to be sectioned off from the general public by means of a large purple curtain and a heavy stone bench. And so, to the casual observer, there were just four Roman Basins and only the museum's staff were ever told about the stash of priceless armaments hidden, just out of sight, in the other two.

However, there was now an exhibit of three rather dog-eared old mannequins that had been found in a skip back in 1983, dug out, carted over and dressed up in the full splendour of Roman Centurions out in the battle field. Each had, up until the day before at least, stood to attention with a sword in one hand and a throwing spear in the other, but after Becky had left, and the Senior Curator had been given a chance to collect his thoughts, he'd noticed that they were all missing their swords and spears; and having forgotten all about the dead security guard now lying underneath the Slaughtered Virgin of Zenopolis, and all the water, he'd called the police.

Sergeant Dewbush was finding that there weren't any direct ways to approach the Roman Basins from Bath City Police Station, so he decided just to drive the wrong way up York Street and save himself the hassle of going around the city's rather elaborate one-way system. Turning the sirens off, he approached the Roman Basins in a relatively sedate manner, and as soon as he'd stopped the car, Capstan and he opened the doors and stepped out.

Looking around for someone awaiting their arrival, but not seeing anyone obvious, Capstan started to wander down towards the Roman Baths, but Dewbush pulled him back and guided him over to the much smaller Basin Museum. Seeing one of its two wooden doors already propped open by a bin, they entered to find themselves inside a good sized but poorly lit lobby that reminded Capstan of the charity shops he used to frequent during his student days, not because the place was stacked to the ceiling with unwanted clutter, or because an old woman sat behind a counter trying to work out how to use a calculator, but because of the smell. It had the same musty, dirty, damp sort of aroma that always greeted him whenever he had the misfortune to enter such a shop.

Still seeing nobody about they took the opportunity to have a good nose around. Neither of them had ever been inside before, not even Dewbush, for even though he'd been born and bred in Bath, and he'd meant to pay a visit, he'd always managed to think up something better to do. So they both roamed the lobby, poking and prodding at the three Centurions, looking at the various leaflets splayed out over the chest-high reception desk and wondering how best to raise awareness of their presence.

'Shall I pop the sirens on, Sir?' Dewbush asked.

'No need! I've found a desk bell,' Capstan said, and

with the palm of his hand, bashed out a hard, resonating ring.

There was a noise of someone falling off a chair behind the reception desk. A young lad popped his head up, looking just a little surprised to see that someone was there. 'Sorry,' he said, rubbing his eyes, 'I must have dozed off. Do you want tickets for the tour?'

'Um, no, not right now thanks, we're actually the police.' For the second time that day Capstan felt it necessary to pull out his formal identification. Dewbush, however, refrained. Frankly he didn't think it was worth the effort and he certainly didn't want to take his notebook out. So he just stood there with his hands in his pockets, gazing about the place a little more.

The young lad, feeling a lot more awake now that he had two real-life policemen standing in front of him, followed suit, shoving both his hands deep into his own pockets to locate the tiny block of hash he kept somewhere down there, just in case he had to ditch it fast. 'Oh, right,' he said, 'I'd better get Mr Hetheringshaw for you then.' He edged his way out from behind the desk and walked backwards through the lobby to disappear behind a faded old red curtain.

'That boy looks like he's stoned out of his tree,' said Capstan quietly. 'I suggest we nick him before we leave.'

'He's probably just tired, Sir.'

Capstan ignored Dewbush's totally un-policeman-like attitude. He was itching to arrest someone and strolled back outside to see if he could find anyone up to something a little more obvious.

A few moments later Dewbush also popped his head outside. 'Excuse me, Sir. The Senior Curator's here now.'

'Oh, very well.' Capstan headed back into the gloomy museum with its rather musty, nostalgic smell.

Dewbush made the introductions. 'Mr Jeffrey Hetheringshaw, this is Inspector Capstan.'

'Are you a police person as well?' asked the old man, already looking confused.

With a sigh, Capstan once again pulled out his formal identification, not knowing that Jeffrey wouldn't have been able to see it even it was lit up with florescent tubing.

'Yes, that's right,' he said. 'I'm Inspector Capstan from Bath City Police. We understand there's been a break-in here.'

'Has there?'

Capstan couldn't help but groan and roll his eyes. It was just going to be one of those days.

'Apparently, yes,' he said. 'A window was forced open and some items were stolen. Does that ring any bells?'

Jeffrey clapped his hands together. 'Yes, that's right! How on earth did you know?'

'It really doesn't matter. Could you just show us exactly what's been stolen?'

'Well, no, sorry. I can't.'

'And may I ask why?'

'Well, I'd like to of course, but they've been stolen. If they hadn't been stolen I'd have gladly shown you. Would you like to take the tour instead? The Roman Basins are really quite something, and far more interesting than the Roman Baths next door.'

'I don't suppose you could tell us what happened first? Then maybe we can take the tour afterwards.'

'Yes of course. Well, it all started when I woke up this morning. I remembered that I'd run out of milk, so I couldn't have my cornflakes like I usually do, so I had to have toast…'

Sensing what was to follow, and not being prepared to listen to the entire rendition of this fascinating character's morning routine, Capstan fast-forwarded him.

'Would it be at all possible for you to start at the part when you noticed something was wrong? Possibly sometime after you'd arrived here, to start work?'

'Well, yes, I suppose I could do.'

They could see he was struggling to remember anything at all, apart from what he'd had for breakfast, so feeling sorry for him, Dewbush tried to help him along.

'You noticed that there was something missing, perhaps?'

'Oh yes, that's right! It was after I'd finished filling up one of our Roman Basins with water, to hide the body of the dead security guard we'd found, the one with the sword sticking out of him. It was then that I noticed that these Centurions here,' and he gesticulated around at the three mannequins, 'had nothing in their hands. But they should have, you see. They should each be holding a Gladius and a Pilum. But as you can see, they're not holding anything at all!'

Capstan and Dewbush were looking at each other. Dewbush slowly pulled out his little black notebook and pen, trying not to distract the old man from his train of thought, and started taking notes.

'That's all very interesting,' Capstan interjected, 'but you mentioned something about a dead security guard, with a sword sticking out of him?'

'Oh, I'd completely forgotten about that. Yes, of course, that was this morning, just before lunch. Becky saw him at the bottom of one of our basins. She thought it would be best if we covered him up, so we threw the Slaughtered Virgin of Zenopolis on top of him and filled the tank up with water.'

Capstan had turned to stare at Dewbush who was already flicking back through his notes. Knowing what they were both thinking, Capstan waited a moment before asking quietly, 'Have you found it yet?'

'Yes, she was called Becky Philips, Sir.'

Capstan looked back to Jeffrey. 'This Becky girl, the one who found the body, it wouldn't happen to be a certain Becky Philips, by any chance?'

'Yes that's right. Clever girl, that one. Works here part-time, you know. Shame really. We could do with someone like her working here permanently. There's always just so much to do.'

'And you said she's also called the Slaughtered Virgin of something?

'The Slaughtered Virgin of Zenopolis?'

'Yes, that's the one!'

'What about her?'

'Is that what she calls herself?'

'Is that what who calls herself?'

'The Slaughtered Virgin of Zenopolis? Is that her… criminal name?'

'I'm not sure the Slaughtered Virgin of Zenopolis has a criminal name, but let me go and check.'

'Hold on, no, sorry, I meant Becky Philips. Is she

known as the Slaughtered Virgin of Zenopolis?'

'Is she? I had no idea!'

'No, I was asking you!'

'Asking me what?'

Capstan took a deep breath. 'Is Becky known as the Slaughtered Virgin of Zenopolis?'

'Not that I know of, but I've always thought they look similar.'

'So, who's that then?' asked Capstan, feeling his brain beginning to melt.

'Who's what?'

'The Slaughtered Virgin of Zenopolis?'

'Oh, that's who we threw on top of the security guard, the one in the basin.'

'But why did you throw Becky on top of the security guard? Was he drowning?'

'No, no, no, not Becky. The Slaughtered Virgin of Zenopolis. It's a statue! Becky threw it on top of the security guard.'

'Oh, I see. And that's how she killed him, was it?'

'How she killed who?'

'The security guard!'

'I don't think I'm feeling very well,' Jeffrey said, sagging visibly. 'Do you mind if I sit down for a moment?'

'Yes, of course you can.'

Capstan didn't feel too good either, and asked Dewbush to pull out a couple of chairs from behind the reception desk.

With them both now sitting, Capstan thought it safe to continue.

'So, do you know how Becky killed the security guard?'

'I'm not exactly sure she did. Did she? The whole thing is becoming rather difficult to remember.'

Feeling that they could probably both do with a break from this rather pointless question and answer routine, Capstan asked, 'I don't suppose we could see where the body is?' Then he added, for clarification, 'The security guard you mentioned.'

'Oh, yes of course. This way. Follow me!' With that, Jeffrey pushed himself out of his chair and was off through the red curtains before they had time to blink.

Taken by surprise by his sudden turn of speed, Capstan and Dewbush pushed the chairs back behind the reception desk and set off after him.

By the time they'd caught up, Jeffrey had already started to bend down to pick up a hose that had been left dangling in a large, cordoned off basin that was full to the brim with water. As he dragged the hose away, Capstan and Dewbush looked down to see that there was indeed something submerged at the bottom, but through the rippling surface it looked like a naked girl copulating with a young man and both enjoying themselves immensely. However, as both human forms were about three feet under water, Capstan had to conclude that at least one of them was dead, so he looked over at Dewbush and said, 'You'd better call everyone, well, everyone who's not either on holiday or down at the bank.'

'Shall I call the fire brigade, Sir?'

'We're not that short staffed, are we?'

'No Sir, to pump out the water.'

'Oh yes, or course, sorry. Very well.'

Dewbush left to make a few calls just as Jeffrey returned.

'Can you see them?' he asked.

'Yes, sort of. We're calling for back up. We're going to have to close the museum down for a while.'

'Are you sure that's really necessary?'

'Yes, I'm afraid so.'

'But with the basin filled up, you can hardly see them, and I'm sure nobody would notice. I've also cordoned off the area as you can see.'

'Even so, it does look like this could be a murder inquiry now, so we'll need full access to the entire museum.'

'Oh, very well then.'

He looked like a broken man and Capstan's heart went out to him.

'But I'm sure it won't be for too long. Maybe just for a few days,' he said, trying to convey empathy, but not doing very well.

'Oh, I suppose so. I'll go and tell the boy that he can take a few days off,' and he trundled away, back down the corridor.

Now on his own, Capstan just stood there, staring down through the water at the ever-fornicating couple. What he really needed was a little time to think, so he decided to leave Dewbush at the museum, giving him a chance to walk back to the station on his own and reflect on the many strange events of the day.

As soon as he'd decided that, he started to think about Becky. How had she managed to pull off a break-in, a murder and an armed robbery, all within what must have been a single twenty-four hour period, and what could have been her motivation for doing so? Then he started to wonder where she was at that precise moment, and what she might be wearing, but he shook his head to re-focus his mind and headed out to find Dewbush and give him his instructions.

CHAPTER VI
REQUIESCE COMEDE BIBE EPULARE
Eat, drink and be merry

BECKY WAS having an interesting sort of a day as well. With no customers to look after, and with no money left to count, Brian had sent them all home early. So she'd headed down to CoffeeBeans on the corner of Stall Street and Westgate Street for some coffee and cake, and settled herself down to watch the world go by for a couple of hours. She really didn't have much else to do. Most of her friends lived either in Bristol, where she grew up, or somewhere else, and the only reason she lived here herself was because she was reading Business at Bath University, and it was far easier for her to find part-time summer work in Bath than it was in Bristol. So, with nobody to hang out with, she just enjoyed a couple of Skinny Lattes and some Carrot Cake, messaged a few people on Facebook, and let her brain rummage around some online fashion shops.

After about an hour she was surprised to receive a call from Jeffrey Hetheringshaw, still down at the Museum. He'd phoned to tell her that she didn't need to come in for a few days. The police had shown up and found the security guard's body, so they'd had to close the museum after all.

Becky was delighted. She didn't tell Jeffrey that,

obviously, and she would miss the money, but of all the jobs she had, it was by far the worst. They were all tediously boring, but that one made the rest feel like a trip to a spa. The job basically involved occasionally showing a few moronically stupid tourists, most of whom couldn't even speak English, three thirty year-old mannequins dressed up as Centurions, some old broken pots, a few statues with their arms missing, two badly painted frescos and four empty Roman Basins. The whole tour only lasted about ten minutes and with nothing else to do she'd have to spend the remaining time either talking to Jack, the boy who worked behind the reception desk who seemed to spend his entire life stoned out of his tree, or worse still, Senior Curator Jeffrey, who seemed to be permanently obsessed with Basins and bloody Roman statues. Furthermore, the whole place smelt awful, just like the inside of a charity shop, and she honestly felt it must be the worst public attraction to have opened its doors since London's very first Flea Circus came to town in 1358 AD, closely followed by the Bubonic Plague.

So, with her restaurant job not starting until seven o'clock, and not wanting to go all the way back to her shared student house, she did what any decent, self-respecting girl would do with a few hours to kill and went shopping. She really needed a new handbag, something bigger than any she currently had, and ideally one with a little light inside that came on automatically whenever she opened it. That way she might actually be able to find something inside it. Large handbags were all very well, and absolutely essential for a girl with three jobs, but they did seem to have more in common with Black Holes than portable storage devices, and she was sick of having to empty it out every time she needed to find her house keys.

Four hours later, having bought herself an immense, cream-coloured leather handbag, and a torch, Becky arrived at Georgeanio's Italian Restaurant on North Parade, opposite the Parade Gardens, to start her third and last job of the day. This was her favourite because she could eat whatever she liked off the menu, without paying for it, and was normally able to consume at least one bottle of wine without anyone noticing during the course of her shift.

Pulling open the restaurant's cute little door, she breezed in and smiled at the waiter as he finished his shift. He was an exceptionally good looking man, but unfortunately completely gay. She squeezed past him as he was taking his last order and whispered, 'Hello' into his ear.

He smiled back at her. Everyone at this little family restaurant liked Becky. What was not to like? She was stunningly attractive, had a great smile, was good with the customers and always arrived on time.

Having also said hello to her boss, Georgeanio himself, she put on her apron, grabbed her notepad and pen, and strolled out to start her four-hour shift. And there she remained for the next two hours, smiling, taking orders, bringing out food and helping herself to the occasional glass of red wine when nobody was looking.

At around 9pm, three young lads walked in off the street, all in high spirits. It was clear that they'd had more than a few beforehand, and they staggered over to a table in a corner before collapsing, grabbing the menus and studying them with great interest, pretending to understand what they said, but none having a clue.

Becky recognised them immediately.

'Hello boys!' she said with a big, warm smile.

All three of them looked up from their menus, grateful for the distraction, and cried, 'BECKY!' in unison, and with only a slight slur. They'd all had a really good laugh when she'd driven them halfway home after the bank job earlier.

'Out celebrating?' she asked.

'That's right,' the shorter one, who she now knew as Mark, said. 'We're all having a great time, thanks to you!'

With that he picked up one of the empty wine glasses, raised it to his fellow robbers-in-arms and toasted, 'To Becky!'

The other two, Sebastian and Johnno, quickly searched around for their own empty glasses and joined in the toast.

'TO BECKY!' and they all attempted to drink the contents of their glasses before realising that there was nothing in them, and then spent several moments looking around the floor, trying to work out where all the wine had gone.

'I'll get you some drinks,' Becky said, amused by their cute, drunken antics, and went off to fetch them a decent bottle of Red.

She strolled back from the bar, cradling a bottle like a baby, and asked, 'So, how much do you think you got then?'

'Well!' Mark replied, placing both elbows on the table. 'We had a quick count and reckon it's at least a million pounds, probably more. Not bad for a day's work, eh lads? Here's to a million pounds!' and they all raised their empty glasses again.

'TO A MILLION POUNDS!' they shouted, before realising that they still didn't have anything to drink.

'That's fantastic, boys, good work!' and she poured them each a glass. 'So, what are you going to spend it all on?'

'Oh, it's for the Roman Imperialists,' Mark said, and with that, and their glasses now full, they raised them once more.

'TO THE ROMAN IMPERIALISTS!' and they proceeded to gulp down the entire contents, as if they were a chart topping boy band who'd only just returned from a four month tour of the Gobi Desert.

Becky had a quick look around and, not seeing any customers with their hands up, took a generous swig from the bottle to finish it off. She was fairly sure the boys weren't going to notice and it wasn't as if they couldn't afford it.

'I'll get you some more,' she said, shaking that one upside down, just to make sure it was empty, and proceeded back to the bar.

She'd returned before they'd even realised she'd gone and plonked three additional bottles down, before pulling up a chair for herself. Feeling much more relaxed, she then started opening the second bottle and continued the conversation.

'So, what are the Roman Imperialists then?'

'That's us!' Mark said, with sudden enthusiasm. 'Well, there's about nine of us in total. We're a Roman Battle Re-Enactment group!'

'Oh, right, I see. So, which battles do you re-enact?'

'We don't really care. It's basically an excuse to get dressed up in Roman Army clobber before bashing the shit out of another group.'

'And that's normal, is it?'

'Oh yes, there are loads of groups in the UK. None as good as us mind, although the one in Bristol is all right, I suppose. They always put up a good fight at least.'

'So, what did you need the money for?'

'Well!' Mark continued, leaning forward and helping himself to some more wine. 'The Bristol lot applied for a grant this year to get some new equipment; armour, shields, swords, that sort of thing, and the buggers were given a thousand pounds! And now they've gone and bought a shed-load of new stuff off E-bay, and if we don't get some new gear ourselves, we're going to have the shit kicked out of us the next time we meet.'

'But why can't you apply for your own grant?'

'We didn't know you could! Anyway, it's too late. The earliest we can now apply is next April, and there's no way we can wait that long. So we thought we'd just rob a bank instead. It's only money after all, and the banks seem to have loads of it!'

Becky had to agree with them.

'Well, keep your heads down, boys. Both the police and the press were round after you left. I wouldn't worry too much about the police, but those reporters are a savage bunch, and you'll be all over the papers tomorrow morning.'

Hearing that, they couldn't help but grin at each other. Just the thought of making it onto the front page of the local newspapers was almost as good as being on X-Factor.

'Do they have any idea who we are?' asked Mark, more out of curiosity than anything else.

'No, not a clue, but make sure you burn that CCTV footage you picked up.'

'Oh, sorry, we've already uploaded it to YouTube.'

'Well, I suggest you take it down again!'

They were a good laugh, and she liked them all, especially Mark, but they really were a few sandwiches short of a picnic.

Becky finished her wine and stood up. 'Anyway, are you ready to order?'

'Can we just have some pizza please?'

'Sure! What type?'

'Pepperoni?'

'Three Pepperoni Pizzas coming right up!'

She then turned around to face the kitchen at the back of the restaurant and yelled, 'THREE PEPPERONI PIZZAS FOR TABLE NUMBER SIX!' and sat back down again.

'When's your next battle?' she asked. She liked the sound of this Roman Army fighting thing.

'Would you like to join?' asked Sebastian.

'Yes, please join us, Becky.' Johnno added. 'You'd be great at it!'

Becky and Mark looked at each other.

'Why not?' she said. 'Count me in!' Seeing another table summoning her, she stood up, drained her glass again, and headed off in just about the right sort of direction.

A few minutes later she was back with the pizzas.

'Here you go, boys, sorry for the wait,' she said as she passed the plates around the table.

Without hesitating, they all tucked in, and while they were totally absorbed by their food, Becky helped herself to some more of their wine. Then she looked around the restaurant again, to see if there was anyone else in desperate need of her help, but as there wasn't, she sat back down.

'I've been thinking.' she said, crossing her legs, swirling her wine around her glass and gazing up at the ceiling. 'You know you said that you need some Roman swords and that sort of thing?'

'Yes,' said Mark, through a mouthful of food. 'Go on.'

'Well, I might know somewhere where you could get hold of some. Rather a lot actually.'

All three boys looked up from their plates, picked up their wine glasses and leant back in their chairs, waiting for her to continue.

'I don't suppose you've heard of the Roman Basin Museum?'

'We've already tried that one,' said Sebastian, followed by, 'Ow!' as Mark kicked him under the table. 'What the fu… what d'ya do that for?'

If Mark was a bit dim, Sebastian was a complete tool. Becky, however, was as sharp as a pointed stick. 'That was you three last night, wasn't it?'

'How do you know about the Roman Basin Museum?' asked Mark.

'Oh, I work there as well, every morning, Monday to Friday. You do know you left a security guard lying at the bottom of a basin with a sword sticking out of him, don't you?'

Mark and Johnno both turned to stare at Sebastian, who just stared back at them innocently before asking,

'What?'

'You know what!' Johnno said.

'Look, I've already told you. He was trying to pull the sword off me, so I just let go, and he stabbed himself with it. Wasn't my fault! And it definitely wasn't my fault that he then decided to walk backwards, straight into one of those stupid basins!'

'Well, you could have been a bit more careful, that's all.'

'Oh, sooorrrrry!' he replied, obviously not feeling very sorry at all.

'I shouldn't worry about it, boys,' Becky interrupted. 'It was only a security guard. Bath's got loads of them!'

The three boys shrugged and carried on filling their mouths up with pizza.

Becky continued, 'So, I suppose you didn't find the Roman armament stash then?'

They all looked back at her again, mouths half full and shaking their heads as they continued to shove in more food.

'At the far end of the main corridor there are two basins closed off to the public. Nobody knows they're there.'

The boys continued to stare at her, but with their mouths now completely full, they just chewed, slowly, like three cows, waiting for the grass to grow.

'They're stacked to the brim with Roman swords, shields, helmets, breast plates, the lot!'

All three stopped chewing and now just stared.

Mark swallowed the contents of his mouth with one huge gulp.

'You're kidding?'

'No! It's a massive haul. They've had it for years.'

'How much have they got?'

'I've no idea, but they've never had enough space to display even a fraction of it. I've had a look a couple of times. It's just all piled up, and it's in mint condition.

'Blimey!' said Mark, looking back at his partners in crime.

Already feeling like a member of the Roman Imperialists, Becky said, 'Well, I suggest we all head back there as soon as possible and borrow it for a while. They won't miss it. They really don't need it and I'm sure they'd rather see it being used as it should be, instead of just piled up in the back of some crappy old museum.'

The three lads thought it was a terrific idea and Mark raised his glass for yet another toast.

'To Becky and the Roman Basin Museum!'

'TO BECKY AND THE ROMAN BASIN MUSEUM!'

Becky laughed and helped herself to some more wine.

Draining her glass, she peered around the restaurant again and noticed another table who must have been waiting for some time, judging by the look on their faces. So she stood up and pointed herself roughly in their direction.

'Back in a sec boys. Customers!' and winked at Mark without realising before staggering over to see what the other diners wanted.

About ten minutes later she weaved her way back. They'd all now finished their pizzas and slouched back in their chairs, chatting happily and trying to wring out a few more drops from the four empty bottles.

'Can I get you anything else?' she offered, pulling out her notepad and pen.

'No, thanks Becky, but we're going to head off. It's been a long day.' Holding onto the table with both hands, Mark carefully pulled himself up.

'OK, no probs. So, when's your next battle meeting?'

'Oh, this Saturday, 10am. Do you know where the University's West Car Park is?'

'Yes! That's where I study.'

'Well, there's a massive park beside it, you know the one. We'll all be meeting there at around ten. Shall we see you then?' asked Mark, doing his best to control both his lips and tongue.

'Absolutely!'

'Good stuff! Er… can we have the bill please?'

'Sure!' she said, and glanced down at everything splayed out over the table. Then she stared thoughtfully up at the ceiling, and finally back at Mark. 'That'll be fifty quid please.'

Mark pulled out an enormous wad of immaculate fifty pound notes. He stared at it for a while, still not quite believing he had it, and then looked at Becky.

'Here you go!' he said and with a big smile, gave the lot to her. 'Keep the change!'

Becky looked down at the huge amount of cash that now lay in her hand; then she looked back at Mark and felt herself becoming extremely aroused. She couldn't work out if it was the cash, or the man. They both looked really good. Anyway, she was too drunk to give it much thought and just smiled back at him and winked again. Mark winked back, and they both looked a little embarrassed at having just given away their mutual interest.

None the wiser to this little courtship, Sebastian and Johnno stood up slowly and both shook Becky's hand with some gusto before heading straight for the door. Mark, being the last to leave, turned back to wave at her.

'See you Saturday then!'

Stuffing the cash straight down her bra, she waved back.

'Yes, see you then, and careful on the way home!'

With that, all three of them weaved their way past the restaurant's window and disappeared out of sight.

Becky looked back at the remaining customers and shrugged. She must have had at least two thousand pounds wedged between her breasts, and she was far too drunk to continue working, so she just took off her apron, threw it over the nearest chair and called out, 'I'll be off then, Georgeanio. Bye!' and walked straight out the door before anyone could question her rather sudden decision to quit..

CHAPTER VII
A COQUINA INTUIT
A kitchen with a view

BECKY AWOKE naturally, rolled over and pulled her smartphone out from under her pillow to check the time.

09:12.

She hadn't woken up that late in ages, and stretched out her entire body with a delicious yawn before rolling over to have another go at sleeping. But she'd never been very good at going back to sleep after waking up, so she just lay there for a while, thinking about Mark, and listening for signs of life in the house as she tried to work out if anyone was using the bathroom.

Becky lived on Milton Avenue in a shared student house, and had done so ever since moving out of Halls of Residence at the end of her first year. Over the summer holidays only two of her housemates had remained, and she knew that, it being Friday, one of them would already be at work. The other was probably either tucked up in bed with his current girlfriend, or had crashed over at her place.

She couldn't hear anyone and, with no particular reason to get up, she just lay there until exactly nine-thirty before dragging herself out of bed for her morning shower.

About fifteen minutes later she strolled out of the bathroom completely naked apart from a fluffy white towel that she'd wrapped around her head. Despite it being a shared house she often did walk around naked, especially in the summer. She had a great body and she knew it. With absolutely no inhibitions and always finding herself sharing a house with men, none of whom had ever complained, she felt free to do as she pleased.

Returning to her bedroom she sat on the edge of her bed and began her routine of applying a liberal amount of moisturising cream over her entire body. Next, she unwrapped the towel from around her head and applied her hair dryer, filling the room with hot, perfumed air. After spending a couple of minutes prodding her dark locks back into some semblance of normality, she decided that what she really needed was a haircut and that that was the very first thing she'd spend some of her recently acquired money on.

As soon as her hair was dry she sat down to sort her face out. She'd only just finished the job, and was still applying the last few strokes of mascara, when there was a loud knock at the front door.

'Coming!' she said to nobody in particular.

Suspecting it was Martin returning from a night out at his girlfriend's house and finding he'd lost his keys again, she walked out of her bedroom and down the stairs, with the mascara bottle in one hand and its brush in the other, and still completely naked.

When she reached the hall she transferred the mascara brush into her left hand and opened the front door.

'Oh look, it's Cat Spam and Bush Dew!' and with one hand resting on the latch she put the other on her naked hip and gave them a completely false smile.

Both Capstan and Dewbush immediately went bright red and desperately tried not to look all over her immaculate porcelain-white body.

'If you want mortgage advice, boys, then you've come to the wrong place.'

Capstan had already forgotten why he was there, but after a few moments his natural police instinct kicked into gear.

'You do know that it's an offence to let yourself be seen in public like this?'

'Then I suggest you sod-off back to wherever it was that you've come from and stop gawping at me like a couple of perverts - or should I call the real police and have YOU arrested?'

'I think we'd better come back later.'

Capstan was already willing to give up. There was just something about this girl that scared the life out of him.

'Oh, for God's sake! Come in then if you have to. I'll put something on,' and she turned around to show them her perfectly formed bum which they happily watched as it headed into the house and back up the stairs.

Capstan and Dewbush remained standing outside the front door. They didn't wish to look at each other. Eventually Capstan cleared his throat and walked inside, making his way along the hallway to wait at the bottom of the stairs. Dewbush followed after him like a horny little pet dog. They were both using their suit jackets to try and hide their rather obvious physical state.

It wasn't long before she appeared again and bounced her way down the stairs as she continued to prod at her hair. She'd hardly got dressed at all. All she'd done was pull on an old boyfriend's light-blue cotton shirt, but hadn't even bothered to do up the buttons, so now she looked even more provocative than she did before.

Capstan didn't dare mention it and just did his best not to allow himself to be completely absorbed by the more than occasional glimpses of her breasts, thighs and just about everything else. Obviously this wasn't possible for either of them, so they just stood there, watching her descend towards them and becoming increasingly aroused with every passing moment. But Capstan did the best that any man could do under such circumstances and continued to use his suit jacket to cover the bulge in his trousers, smiling at her courteously as she brushed passed him on her way to the kitchen.

'Would you like a coffee, boys?' she called out behind her.

At this point, anything to help distract them from their current predicament was welcome.

'Er, yes please, thank you. That would be nice,' they muttered, and followed her down the narrow hallway.

Becky filled up the kettle, popped it on and started to take out an assortment of items from the cupboards and fridge to make some drinks for her uninvited guests. And as she reached both up and down, Capstan and Dewbush would steal as many glances as possible without risking being caught, and without letting each other know what they were up to.

'So what's this all about then?' Becky asked as she grabbed a tea spoon and opened up a jar of instant coffee.

It was only then that Capstan remembered that when he'd woken up that morning his intention was to take her straight down to the station for questioning. Now he found himself in the middle of her kitchen, watching her gorgeous near-naked body make him some coffee. He certainly didn't mind the view, but it was hardly the best place to begin an interrogation, so he pulled out the Daily Bath from under his arm and placed it on the kitchen table.

'Have you seen the newspapers today?' he asked, congratulating himself on having found the perfect way to kick things off without antagonising her any more than was necessary.

'No! I don't read newspapers,' she answered absently, as the kettle boiled and she began pouring its contents into the three very student-like mugs that were lined up on the counter. 'I can't say I watch the news either.'

She added in some milk to each, deliberately not bothering to ask them how they liked it, and continued.

'I've always thought that if something happens that I really need to know about, someone will tell me.'

Capstan and Dewbush shrugged. That did seem to make perfect sense. Anyway, Capstan thought he'd better get the ball rolling.

'Have you heard that the Basin Museum was broken into the night before last, and that a security guard was found dead?'

He couldn't wait to see how she'd respond to that one.

Becky turned around to face them, and they were reminded that she still had absolutely nothing on under her shirt.

'Listen boys, you probably already know that I work at the Basin Museum as well as the bank, and that I did help to throw a statue on top of a security guard, but I only did it because I was late for my shift at the bank, and the guy was already dead, so I didn't think he'd mind too much.'

Capstan chose his next words very carefully.

'So, you're saying that you didn't have anything to do with the Basin Museum break-in, the murder of the security guard, or the bank job. Is that correct?'

'I know it sounds odd, but no, I didn't! I just happened to be doing a tour when we found the security guard, and then I turned up at the bank when it was being robbed. Apart from helping to throw the statue on top of that dead guy, I had nothing to do with either.'

'Can you at least tell us where you dropped off the three bank robbers?'

'Yes, it was at the top of Bathwick Hill.'

'Did you see which way they went after that?'

'No, they just waved goodbye and I drove back into town.'

'Do you think you'd recognise them if you saw them again?'

'Oh sure, I actually saw them last night!'

He was finally onto something. She'd clearly slipped up, so he jumped in with his next question.

'And where exactly did you meet them?'

'I didn't meet them, they just showed up at the restaurant where I work.'

Capstan now found himself trying to keep up with this girl's rather busy work schedule as well as the many complexities of the case.

'Right! So how often do you work at the restaurant?'

'Every evening, Monday to Friday.'

'And why were they at the restaurant where you just happened to be working?'

'I'm not sure. Probably to celebrate.'

He put one hand on his forehead and rubbed it with some vigour. Then he looked at Dewbush, who'd been trying to take notes for some time, but hadn't been doing a very good job.

'May I sit down?' he asked. He thought this would at least allow him to stop worrying about trying to hide what he felt had become a permanent erection and focus on the interview, as best he could.

'Sure, help yourself,' she said, turning back to grab the steaming hot mugs from off the counter.

Dewbush needed to sit down as well, and so they both screeched out a couple of white wooden chairs from under the kitchen table and sat with no small amount of relief.

Now that Capstan was feeling less exposed he was able to digest the new piece of information about the restaurant. Making a mental note to himself to remain calm and not let this girl's flippant attitude to just about everything wind him up, he continued.

'Can you tell me the name of this restaurant where you work?'

She brought the mugs over and placed them on the kitchen table.

'It's called Georgeanio's, on North Parade, opposite Parade Gardens. Do you know it?'

He did, but he wasn't going to be side-tracked quite

so easily.

'And what time was it when they arrived there to, er… "celebrate"?'

'Oh, it must have been around nine o'clock. Something like that.' She headed back to the counter to pop some bread in the toaster. 'Do you want anything to eat?'

'No, thank you, we're fine with the coffee, thanks. Did they mention anything to you about the robbery?'

'Oh yes, they were all very excited about it.'

'And did they tell you that they'd gotten away with over a million pounds?'

'Yes, they did. Why, is that a lot?' she asked, pulling out some butter and jam from the fridge.

'Well, it's quite a lot, yes.' replied Capstan, with increasing incredulity.

'You know,' said Becky, as she stopped what she was doing to gaze around the kitchen, 'this place is probably worth about half that, so it's not that much really, is it?'

Again, they both had to agree with her.

Capstan looked down at the newspaper that Becky hadn't even glanced at yet. He had no idea what to ask her now. He was convinced that she was up to her neck in the whole thing, if for no other reason than the fact that she'd been at the museum, the bank and now at the restaurant, all at exactly the same time, or as near to it as she was prepared to admit, as the three other suspects had. It was just beyond coincidental. But the way she talked about the whole thing, it really did seem as if she was completely innocent.

'I don't suppose they told you where they lived, by any chance?'

He was now grasping at straws.

'No, sorry.'

Then he had an idea.

'Did they pay by credit card?'

'No, cash!' she replied, smiling to herself as she popped the toast out and started to apply the butter and jam.

He was back to square one again.

'Maybe you can describe them for us?'

'Yes, sure. Let me think.' She took the first bite of her toast, turned to face them and leaned back against the counter. 'They were all men, they were white, and young, in their early twenties, just under six feet tall, vaguely attractive, and they all had short, light-brown hair.'

'So they looked very similar to just about every other young white-male living in the UK then?'

He couldn't help add the sarcasm.

'I guess so,' she replied and folded her arms to continue eating her toast whilst staring at Capstan. She knew he was getting absolutely nowhere and was enjoying playing with him. So, just for fun, she thought she'd throw him a bone.

'Oh, and I know their names as well!'

Both policemen perked up.

'Go on,' said Capstan, impatiently as Dewbush poised himself with his pen.

'They're called Mark, Sebastian and, er… Fred I think, or was it Jacob?'

Capstan groaned.

'Did they tell you their surnames by any chance?'

'No, sorry, I didn't think to ask.'

He rubbed his forehead again with increasing

frustration.

'I don't suppose that at any time between when they waltzed into the restaurant, where you just happened to be working, and when they waltzed back out again, you thought it might be a good idea to call the police?'

'No, not really.'

They both stared at her with their mouths open, but as neither of them seemed to be able to follow that one up with another question, she thought she'd say something more, to keep the game going a little longer.

'Well, I can't see why I should have. They weren't wearing masks or anything, and they didn't have their guns with them. They just sat down and ordered pizza. Why would I have called the police?'

'I don't know either,' Capstan answered, becoming increasingly pissed off, 'but maybe because all three are wanted for armed robbery and were out celebrating, having only just held up the very bank where you happen to work, and from where they'd walked away with over a million pounds, in cash?'

'Well yes, but what do I care? I don't exactly have an account with the Instathon.'

'AH-HA!' Capstan exclaimed, somewhat over-dramatically. 'The Bank Manager said that all staff members had accounts there, isn't that so Dewbush?'

Dewbush jumped in his chair. He hadn't been listening to anything for ages as he'd just been sitting there, transfixed by Becky's unashamed nakedness. But realising that perhaps he should have been, he started leafing through the pages of his notebook, hoping that his boss would think that he was looking for the answer to whatever it was that he'd just been asked.

Becky was a little surprised to see Capstan becoming so excited, but she continued talking to him in very much the same way as she had been doing ever since they'd shown up outside the front door.

'Yes of course, we've all got accounts there, but I've never put any money into it. The Instathon Bank is rubbish. I wouldn't trust them with my pants, let alone my money!'

Capstan was beginning to wonder if Becky did actually own a pair of pants, or if she had them all locked away in a top secret military vault somewhere. But feeling that he'd again been completely defeated, he just sat there and stared at her body, without caring what anyone thought; and seeing what Capstan was doing, Dewbush did the same.

Realising that they were now both openly ogling her, Becky thought she'd play along. So she went back to the sink, gave her hands a quick wash and walked over to the nearby clothes rack that stood in front of the radiator. She then casually slipped her shirt off over her shoulders and threw it into the washing machine. Now, completely naked, she picked up a pair of tiny white knickers from off the rack and stepped into them, as slowly as she could without losing her balance. Then she picked up a very small pink t-shirt and squeezed herself into it, pulling it down as far as it would go so that it clung tightly to her breasts. Considering herself now to be fully dressed, she stepped over to the kitchen table, where both men still sat with their mouths hanging open, and picked up their two half-empty coffee mugs.

'If there's nothing else boys, I'd really appreciate it if you could run along now. I've got a hair appointment in half an hour.'

She hadn't arranged it yet, but was about to.

There was no reply. So she put the coffee mugs into the sink and turned around to stare directly at them with both hands on her hips.

Capstan and Dewbush really didn't want to go anywhere. The view from where they were sitting was just far too good, and the idea of standing up in their current state wasn't appealing.

'Can you both please go now?' she asked, with fabricated impatience. She knew exactly what their predicament must be, and had no intention of letting them off lightly. Besides, she was looking forward to watching them both try to stand up after the performance she'd just put on for them.

They cleared their throats. There was nothing for it. They were going to have to get up, and so they both desperately started trying to think of something that might help to deflate their current, all too embarrassing situation, but nothing came to mind. In fact the only two things that did keep coming to mind were both being pushed out at them from behind a pink t-shirt that looked as if it was about to burst with bountiful goodness.

Unable to think of anything less sexually arousing, Capstan just grabbed the copy of Bath Daily from off the table which he then used to cover himself up with.

Dewbush, now cursing himself for not having bought his own copy, just stood up and used his suit jacket again.

'Thanks boys, and thanks for coming around. I hope I was able to be of some help at least; and do feel free to come back again, any time you like.'

Wishing he'd never been born, Capstan followed Dewbush out into the narrow hall, deliberately keeping his back to the girl.

'Yes, well, thank you for your time, Miss Philips, and no doubt we'll be back in touch.'

Dewbush also wanted to show his appreciation, so he added, 'Yes, thank you Becky. Thank you very much!'

He really had enjoyed the interview and sincerely hoped he would be able to come back again, but preferably on his own next time, and maybe with a bottle of wine and a packet of condoms.

Inside Capstan was fuming. He'd never been so embarrassed in all his life, and having his Sergeant now openly flirting with the suspect really wasn't helping.

Dewbush opened the door and invited his boss to step out first, so he could have another chance to see Becky, but Capstan knew exactly what he was up to and gave him a look that cleared Dewbush's mind of just about everything accept being able to pay his next month's rent. So he stepped out first, and left Capstan to it.

Before walking out the door, and feeling slightly more in control of himself, Capstan turned back to face her.

'We will be back with some more questions Miss Philips, so please don't think about going anywhere,' and forced a thin smile at her.

'Can't wait, but do call ahead next time. I might be in the bath!' and she winked at him.

She enjoyed winking at men. She found it always had some sort of a reaction.

Capstan blushed again, and was furious with

himself for doing so. He then turned to head out after Dewbush, who'd already wandered off down the street to find their car.

Becky continued to watch them until they were out of sight before closing the door. She knew she'd been very naughty, but it was all just far too much fun, and they both fully deserved everything they got - well, Capstan did anyway. He was just such a spanner.

With that, she forgot all about them and went back up to her bedroom to continue thinking about Mark and their next rendezvous the following day at 10am. Between now and then she had some serious shopping to do.

CHAPTER VIII
DOMINA EST, NEQUE ENIM OGLING
The lady's not for ogling

AS THEY MADE their way back down Becky's street to their car parked on the adjoining road, Capstan still seethed, but Dewbush had a completely different look about him, almost as if he was in love.

'I'll drive!' said Capstan, which woke Dewbush up. He'd always thought of it as his car, but then remembered the look Capstan had given him when leaving Becky's house and threw the keys over.

They set off at a tire squeaking pace and headed straight back towards the police station. Neither of them spoke. Capstan was busy planning ways to exact his revenge on Becky, which varied from having her spanked to death to lining her up in front of a firing squad wearing nothing more than a blindfold. Meanwhile, Dewbush was also thinking about her, and although he wouldn't have minded giving her a jolly good spanking, he was more preoccupied with how he could get back to her place to re-enact the interview that they'd just had, except without his boss being there, and skipping all the boring question and answer stuff. With such a hedonistic liaison in mind, and not much else, he asked his boss, 'Do you think she meant that, the bit about us coming back, whenever we liked?'

Capstan ignored him.

Another few minutes of silence passed before Dewbush piped up again.

'I don't suppose you've got her phone number?'

Capstan slammed on the brakes and the car screeched to a rather dramatic halt, forcing the three cars behind to do something similar. He looked over at Dewbush and, through gritted teeth and a seething snarl, said, 'If I hear you mention that woman's name in my presence again you'll be working as a lollypop man before the week's out!'

When the three cars behind them started beeping with annoyance, Capstan felt a surge of fury growing inside of him that he wasn't sure he could control. As he began to transform into a cross between the Incredible Hulk and Inspector Gadget, he reached over to pull his hand gun out from the glove box, stepped out of the car and then walked up to the vehicle directly behind him. Arriving at the driver's window he tapped on the glass with the gun and showed the man sitting there his Police ID before politely asking him to wind the window down. It was fairly obvious that the driver didn't want to do anything of the sort, but wasn't sure he had much choice. When the window was fully open, Capstan smiled at him, shoved the gun down into his groin and whispered, 'If you beep that bloody horn again, I'll blow your fucking knob off!'

He then stood up and snarled back at the other two drivers. Judging by the look on their faces Capstan felt satisfied that they'd all learnt a valuable lesson. He wasn't sure what that lesson was, but he was confident that they'd learnt it, so he swaggered back to his own car.

Once he'd sat down in the driver's seat he pulled the door closed, threw his gun back into the glove box and was instantly struck by a brilliant idea. He looked directly at Dewbush and smiled. This completely freaked Dewbush out. Having only just witnessed his boss threaten a fellow road user with what he assumed must have been a public execution, simply for beeping his horn, there was no telling what he was capable of. Fortunately for Dewbush, Capstan just slipped the car into first and set off again, following the one-way system around with a demonic look about him.

At the next set of lights Capstan asked Dewbush, 'What shoe size are you?' as if passing the time of day.

Dewbush was more than a little thrown by the question, not because it was particularly difficult, but because he couldn't understand its relevance to anything at all. The only thing he could think that it might have a bearing on was starting a new job as a lollypop man, and that Capstan needed to order him some special shoes.

'Um, I'm a size eight, Sir.'

Capstan soon saw what he was looking for and pulled over to illegally park on the curb.

'Stay here!' he ordered, stepped out of the car and headed straight into the Charity Shop opposite.

About ten minutes later he came out carrying a large white plastic bag. He walked right up to Dewbush's door and opened it.

'Get in the back and put this lot on!'

Without hesitation, Dewbush stepped out of the car, took the bag and climbed into the back. Peering inside he found what seemed to be a pink flowery dress, a brown curly wig, some large sunglasses and a pair of old stilettos.

When Capstan sat back behind the wheel Dewbush asked, 'You must be joking Sir?' more out of shock than anything else.

'I'm not bloody joking! Now you're going to put that lot on and I'm going to drive you back to that woman's house. Then you're going to follow her! I want to know her exact movements; where she goes, what she does, what she eats, drinks, absolutely bloody everything, but especially who she talks to! If I'm not very much mistaken she'll lead you straight to her little band of brothers and we'll have them all locked up before tea time.'

And with that he set off to re-join Bath's rather elaborate one-way system.

It then dawned on Dewbush that he'd just been given a direct order to follow Becky around for the entire day, and he beamed with delight. He took one more look inside the bag before dumping it on the seat beside him and pulling off all his clothes.

Within five minutes he'd managed to undergo a metamorphosis, from a mild-mannered police sergeant to a slightly drunk-looking femme fatale, blessed with wide shoulders, good bone structure and a light dusting of stubble.

Reaching the end of the street adjoining Becky's again, Capstan parked up, well out of sight of her house. He then turned back to look at Dewbush and was pleasantly surprised. Dewbush made a remarkably convincing woman. Yes, it may have been better if he'd shaved first, and they hadn't had a chance to buy any makeup, but even so, he did look like a girl, all things considered.

Delighted with his newly thought-up covert operation, Capstan said, 'Right, give me your Police ID - I don't want to be associated with any of this. But take your phone with you. Tell you what, put all your normal clothes into the charity bag and take that too. It'll make you look more like you're out shopping.'

Dewbush, somewhat self-consciously, stepped out of the car.

'Report to me on the hour, every hour, or just as soon as she makes contact with them; and most important of all, don't let her out of your sight!'

'Yes, Sir!' Dewbush replied with another huge grin, and watched Capstan reverse back down the street, do a three-point turn and disappear in a cloud of exhaust fumes.

Dewbush inched up to the end of the road and peered around the corner, where he could just about see Becky's house. There were no signs of life and so he just stood there and waited.

Time plodded by, and as it did so he began to feel increasingly conspicuous, hoping to God that he didn't see anyone he knew or, more importantly, anyone who knew his Mum. Then he thought of something that even his boss hadn't considered. What if Becky went somewhere by car? He'd hardly be able to run after her, not in stilettoes anyway. And what if she drove off up the A4?

He was just beginning to have misgivings about the whole enterprise when he heard a front door slam. Easing his head around the corner he saw her, bouncing over the road and heading straight for him, wearing nothing more than a virtually transparent summer dress that left nothing to his already over-stimulated imagination. Such a sight would have made any heterosexual man stare, wide-eyed and mouth agog, but she wasn't even wearing a bra; and she was a big girl. It took all Dewbush's many years of police training to pull himself back behind the corner before being spotted, but having now become aroused all over again he found himself in a very serious situation; he was wearing a dress, a garment never designed to be worn by people with huge, uncontrollable erections. He decided that he had two clear choices; either to hang his plastic bag off it and freeze, so pretending to be some sort of perverted human statue, or to turn around and pretend to search for some keys inside his bag, whilst doing his best to think about something from his past that would help to deflate him, like the time his Mum had made him use the three second rule after he'd dropped his ice cream onto a big pile of poo. He went for the latter, and just in time too, as at that moment she walked straight past him, seemingly unaware of his very existence.

He watched her over his shoulder as she passed. The view of her behind was even more appealing than her front. The dress she'd chosen did little to hide anything at all, and her thin white pants only served to accentuate her perfect form. So, before he realised it, he was staring at her all over again, and all thoughts of having to eat an ice cream covered in poo were, once more, but a distant memory.

So without further ado he set off after her, with scant regard for what anyone might think about his somewhat unusual choice of wardrobe, especially when coupled with his undisguised manhood prominently displayed out before him.

And so it was that Dewbush lolloped along after Becky's bum, as it swayed erotically in front of his eyes, like a sex-therapist's watch being used to induce a deep hypnotic trance. Subsequently he didn't think about looking both ways whenever he had to cross a road, forcing a number of drivers to brake hard to prevent him from being spattered on their bonnets and getting his wig tangled up in their windscreen wipers. But Dewbush was oblivious to all of this as he only had eyes for the girl in front of him.

He continued along like this all the way into Bath's main shopping area where Becky eventually headed into Bettany's Department Store. Naturally Dewbush just followed straight in after her, but as soon as he entered, the spell was broken, and he realised he'd have to be more careful now that she'd stopped walking in a straight line. So, from a safer distance he proceeded to observe her weave and bob around the entire ground floor, stopping at one rack to unhook something, and then holding it up in the air, thoughtfully, before placing it back and moving to the next. Dewbush tried hard to keep behind her as best he could, to reduce the chance of being seen, but he occasionally found himself having to dive behind a rack of clothes when she turned around unexpectedly to gaze over in his general direction.

It was during one such moment when he remembered that he was supposed to call his boss on the hour, every hour and had completely forgotten about it, so he pulled out his phone.

'Hello,' he whispered, 'Dewbush here. Yes, sorry. I forgot. As we speak, yes, Sir. I followed her all the way into town and she's now in Bettany's. It may be that she's going to meet them here. Right, yes, Sir. No, I won't take my eyes off her. OK, bye then,' and he hung up to continue his clandestine surveillance operation.

About twenty minutes later, and still not having picked out anything from the many hundreds of items on offer, Becky had made her way into the Lingerie Department. It was there that she finally found some items that must have taken her fancy, as she carried them straight into the lady's changing rooms. Keen to follow his orders to the letter, Dewbush grabbed a couple of bras off the nearest rack and took off after her.

He was just in time to see her step into one of the changing cubicles on the left hand side. As soon as he saw its yellow curtains close behind her, he tip-toed down to where she was and, finding the opposite cubicle empty, ducked inside. He then hung up the bras and closed the curtains before easing them open, just enough to peer through the gap. He couldn't believe it. She'd hardly bothered to close her curtains at all, and he could see her, plain as day, wriggling herself out of her already unzipped dress. Gripping the curtains tightly, he watched her slip it all the way down before stepping out of it and bending over to pick it up. She then proceeded to take off her tiny white pants before standing, completely naked once again, to admire herself in the mirror.

It was just all too much for Dewbush and he gave in to the extraordinarily fortunate circumstances he seemed to have found himself in. So he lifted up his own dress, pulled down his boxer shorts and used one hand to grab hold of himself and the other to keep the curtain open. Then he fixed his eyes on her as she stepped into the first set of lingerie, a lacy black, one-piece basque that accentuated her every curve to perfection. When she seemed happy that it was all on properly, she turned around and stuck her bum out at the mirror, to have a look at the rear view. Then she turned back around and pushed her breasts out, to make sure it looked equally good from the front. Dewbush then watched her slowly peal it off, bending over so that her bum pointed directly at him, out through her half-opened curtains. He couldn't hold back any longer and came at full volume, but at that precise moment his curtains flew open and there stood a huge, Hispanic-looking female security guard.

'WHAT THE HELL DO YOU THINK YOU'RE DOING!' she shouted, with utter contempt.

The combined force of his ejaculation, and the shock of having a vision of Becky replaced by the Spanish inquisition in female form, sent him flying backwards, at which point his wig and sunglasses fell off.

Hearing the commotion, Becky pulled back her curtains and stood there, completely naked once again, staring at Dewbush as he scrambled about like a rat cornered inside an industrial sized wheelie bin. She'd known he'd been spying on her ever since she'd left her house. He hadn't exactly been difficult to spot; after all, it had probably been the first time she'd ever seen such an obvious transvestite hanging around a street corner in Bath, and she'd certainly never seen one with such a huge erection before. So she'd delighted herself in the task of playing with him like a pussycat toying with a mouse. But it was now time for the kill and she clutched at both her ample breasts and screamed, just about as loudly as she could.

That should do it, she thought.

Now seeing exactly what had been going on the great, hulking security guard grabbed Dewbush by his hair and dragged him, kicking and screaming, with his boxers around his ankles, his right hand holding the guard's wrist and the other covering his still ejaculating knob. By this time a couple of sales assistants had also run in to see what was going on and as the guard dragged him past them she said, 'Call the police, I've caught myself a Peeping Tom!'

As Dewbush disappeared out of the changing room, Becky waived goodbye to him and smiled wickedly to herself.

'One down, one to go,' she said, and although she did feel just a little sorry for him, it wasn't her fault that he'd decided to dress up like a girl, follow her into the lady's changing rooms and masturbate to the sight of her getting undressed. He might even have got away with it too, if it wasn't for all the moaning and groaning he'd been doing, especially towards the end, but she did find herself feeling guilty. He was a sweet, good-looking boy, and probably didn't deserve it, so she promised to make it up to him at some point in the near future.

But with the game now over she returned to the difficult task of making up her mind about the outfit and considered which one Mark would prefer; the black one-piece basque or the thong and lace bra. She couldn't decide, so instead she wondered which one he'd find easier to take off, and with that she picked up the thong and bra, and started to get dressed again. And as she did so she mused over just how long it might be before she managed to create the opportunity to show Mark her new purchase; probably not the next morning, but maybe later that evening? She'd have to think about it whilst having her hair done, but she was going to have to get a wiggle on. After her hair she needed a manicure, and she still hadn't decided what she'd be wearing for her first meeting with the Roman Imperialists the very next day.

CHAPTER IX
ALTERI BELLO
Fight another day

SITTING AT HIS desk, Capstan cradled his head in his hands and stared down at a blank pad of paper. Standing in front of him was a dejected-looking Dewbush, who also looked down, but at the floor, not at the desk, and in shame, not in anger and wholehearted disappointment.

Capstan looked up at him. He still wore the charity shop dress, wig, and sunglasses, but now held the stilettoes in one hand and the charity shop's bag in the other. Remarkably, he still looked like a femme fatale, but now more like one who'd been poisoned, beaten, strangled, stabbed, and shot, before being buried in a ditch and then dug up again.

Looking back down at his desk he found himself desperate to laugh at Dewbush, but he was far too cross. Eventually, having regained his composure, he looked up and said, 'I blame myself, Dewbush. I shouldn't have sent you out alone, not against that… woman. You're no match for her. I'm not sure anyone is!'

'Yes, Sir. No, Sir,' replied Dewbush, still staring at the floor.

'And you're very lucky, believe it or not. When they found out you were a policeman on special assignment, they didn't want to press charges. But this is your very last chance Dewbush, and to be honest, if we weren't so short-staffed, and if the Chief Inspector wasn't drifting about on a yacht somewhere in the Mediterranean, then you'd be out on your ear. Look, let's put the whole thing behind us. Anyway, I need you!'

'Yes, Sir. Thank you, Sir.'

'Right, well then, pull up a chair and take that bloody wig off!'

'Yes, Sir. Of course, Sir.'

'And cheer up for Christ's sake, we've got work to do!'

'Yes, Sir. Right away, Sir.'

'OK, let's have a think. What have we got so far?'

Picking up his pen, Capstan started scrawling on the pad in front of him.

'We know that the Basin Museum was broken into sometime during the night of Wednesday the fourteenth, and that two swords and three spears were stolen. We also know that a third sword was found sticking out of a security guard. Now, while you've been out on your, er, doing your, um,' - Capstan didn't want to mention Dewbush's assignment again - 'thing, the forensics report came back on the security guard's body. Unfortunately it's worse than useless.'

He reached down, picked it out of the bin where he'd thrown it, and handed it to Dewbush.

'As you can see, the cause of death is inconclusive. It could have been the sword, the fall into the basin, the statue thrown on top of him, or the five tonnes of water that he was submerged under. The bottom line is that there is no accurate cause of death, and as the body was under water for such a long time, there are no fingerprints, and no DNA samples. It's a complete dead end!'

'Could we not arrest her for perverting the course of justice, for when she tried to hide the body?'

'Well, not really, no! From what I can work out, it was the tourists who suggested the idea about throwing something on it, and then filling the basin up. Becky seemed happy just to play along. And we can't very well arrest a bunch of tourists; we'd have the Foreign Office on our backs before we'd had a chance to make them all a cup of tea!'

'Yes, I suppose you're right, Sir.'

'Of course I'm bloody right!'

Capstan rubbed his forehead with his hand with some vigour, as he had a habit of doing when under pressure.

'The bank robbery took place at around one pm on Thursday. There were no discernible fingerprints picked up, they only took unmarked bills, the CCTV footage was removed and the only witness who saw their faces was the one who gave them a lift home!'

'Halfway home, Sir.'

Capstan glowered at Dewbush.

'Sorry, Sir.'

'And then Miss Philips,' Capstan spoke her name as if spitting poison, 'met them all again at the restaurant that evening, where she just happened to be working, and when questioned about the whole bloody thing she didn't seem to think they'd done anything wrong!'

Dewbush sat there silently and let Capstan plough on.

'Becky's the key, I know she is! It's just all too much of a coincidence, her being at the museum, the bank and the restaurant, but I'm buggered if I know how to prove it.'

Dewbush was about to suggest that maybe he could follow her again but, fortunately for him, changed his mind.

'Any ideas, Dewbush?'

'None at all, Sir. Sorry, Sir.'

Pushing his chair back, Capstan stood up and started pacing around the room. He found it easier to think when he was walking, not that he ever found it easy to think, but he did find it slightly less difficult when he was moving around.

'Maybe we could find a police woman to keep tabs on her?' he mumbled to himself. 'But knowing Becky, she'd probably seduce her too!'

He continued pacing with his hands clenched behind his back.

'Perhaps we could use a whole surveillance team? That way they could keep an eye on her, and each other, at the same time,' he mused. 'But then she'd probably find some way to get them all naked and bonking each other in some sort of mass police orgy!'

Walking back to his chair, Capstan sat down, picked up his pen again and tapped it on the pad. The only thing he'd written was "Becky", so he underlined it. Then he looked up at the ceiling, rubbed his chin, stared back at the pad and added a large exclamation mark.

'It's no good, Dewbush. The only sensible thing I can come up with is that we pull back and let her think that we've given up. Hopefully that will give her enough rope to hang herself with, and then, when she does make a mistake, we can arrest her.'

'Yes, Sir. Sounds like a good idea, Sir.'

'Well I hope so, I really do. Look, it's Friday. Go home and take the weekend off. Let's meet back here again at nine on Monday morning. Maybe something will come up over the weekend that will give us something to work with.'

'Yes, Sir. Thank you, Sir,' he said, but didn't move.

'Well, bugger off then for Christ's sake!'

'Oh, sorry Sir. Right away, Sir.'

'And make sure you change out of those bloody clothes before you leave. I think we've all had quite enough excitement for one day, don't you?'

'Yes, Sir. Of course, Sir,' and with that Dewbush pushed himself out of the chair and padded out towards the door.

'I'll see you on Monday then, Sir?'

But there was no response from Capstan who was too busy underlining the name "Becky" again, so Dewbush snuck out and headed downstairs for a much needed shower and to change back into his more traditional attire.

CHAPTER X
I ASPICERE VELLET BONUM SUPER VOS
I'd look good on you

BECKY STEPPED out of her little yellow Mini Cooper on what was another fine summer's morning. She was early, as always, but could already see Mark, along with a few others, all hanging around the back of a rather manky-looking white van with its rear doors open.

Unusually for her she was nervous, but was at least confident in her final outfit choice; tight blue jeans, solid brown leather two-inch heeled boots, and a short khaki-green combat jacket that she couldn't do up even if she wanted to. But the fact that it was at least two sizes too small for her meant that it gave full coverage to her bright orange t-shirt that had, "I'd look good on YOU!" stamped on it in black with a strong, military style font. She'd discovered it in a small boutique shop on Westgate Street and had bought it without hesitation, thinking it would save a lot of faffing about if she could make her interest known to Mark without the possibility of being misunderstood.

She was also thrilled with her new hair style that to her was radically different, but to any man probably looked exactly the same as the old one. Whether or not it was worth the ninety-five pounds she paid for it was debatable, but she was pleased and it was certainly helping to bolster her confidence.

Glancing at her reflection in the car's side window she took a deep breath, licked her immaculate white teeth, and turned to stride up towards the van and the young men gathered behind it.

As she approached she called out, 'Hello boys!' with her usual sensual charm. They all turned to stare over, in awe of such resplendent beauty. Her combat-ready loveliness would have been difficult for any man to resist. Mark was especially pleased to see her. He'd been thinking about her, and probably more than was good for him.

'Hello, Becky, you look fantastic!'

She beamed with delight at such an unreserved vote of approval. Looking deep into his eyes, she smiled and said, 'Thank you, Mark. You don't look so bad yourself!' Then she ran both her hands up through her hair to tie it up at the back, so giving him a full, unobstructed view of the message stamped all over her breasts.

He blushed a little, made a note of both her body language and the language on her body, and cleared his throat before making some formal introductions.

'Becky, this is Adam and Carl. You already know Sebastian and Johnno. Over there,' he pointed at a group she hadn't noticed before who were busy either strapping various pieces of Roman armour on, or using their swords to stab at the air with malicious, if not pointless, intent, 'are Mike, Kevin and Luke. The rather large one on the end is Doughnut.'

'Why's he called Doughnut?'

Mark gave her a sideways glance, not expecting her to have asked such an obvious question.

'Because his first name's Duncan!'

She put her stupidity down to nerves and pushed on.

'So, what are you all up to today?'

'Oh, just the normal battle training. We get all our gear on and practice some set moves, that sort of thing. Let me give you the tour.'

About three and a half minutes later the tour was over and they were back where they'd started from. All they'd done was walk around the van.

'So, despite having over a million pounds in cash, you've only got this crappy old van, six swords, a few throwing spears, some dented pieces of armour, eight shields and nine active members?'

Feeling defensive Mark replied, 'Yes, but the Bristol lot only has seven!'

'But it's hardly an army though, is it? You may be able to defeat Belgium but you'd have a tough job with France! You must at least be able to buy some more equipment?'

'We had hoped to, but the Bristol lot already bought the batch being sold by a local film production company. We are bidding for some stuff on eBay, but it's going to take a while to see if we get it.'

'What are you bidding on?'

'Oh, a sword, another full set of Roman armour and a Spartacus DVD box set.'

'Is that it?'

'Um, yes. There really isn't all that much for sale at the moment.'

'So why on Earth did you rob the bank then?'

'Er, well, we thought we'd only get a few grand. We didn't realise they'd have quite so much money!'

'But they're a bank! What did you think they'd have an abundance of - milk?'

Mark looked hurt and she realised her attempt at humour probably came over as being overly offensive, so she changed the subject.

'Anyway, how about showing me some of your moves?'

His expression then changed from one of dejection to acute embarrassment and glanced down at her t-shirt again. He wasn't exactly sure what she'd meant by that and, although keen to suggest a location along with a few positions, he thought he'd better wait for further clarification before doing so.

Realising that she'd probably been misunderstood, she smiled at him, brushed one hand through her hair and said, 'Maybe later for that, but I meant your battle moves!'

'Oh!' Mark said, with some relief, 'Yes, of course!' and he turned around and bellowed out, 'Right men, line up! Let's do some drills.'

There was a metallic rattling sort of a noise, like a box of empty baked bean cans being tipped out into a recycling bin, as the eight soldiers in front of them formed up in to two lines of four, some with swords and some holding spears, but all wearing full armour and carrying large rectangular Roman shields.

'Alright men, Shell Position!'

With that, they moved closer together before the four at the front crouched down and planted their shields next to each other. At the same time the four at the back attempted to lift their shields up over the men in front, but Doughnut misjudged the gap and whacked Sebastian over the head.

'Ow! For fuck's sake Doughnut, that really hurt!'

'Poor thing! Serves you right for being such a pussy!'

'Right, shut up you lot.' Mark stepped forward and attempted to regain control of his band of brothers. 'Doughnut, you need to be able to do that without taking Sebastian's head off.'

There was a mumbled apology from the big man at the back.

'OK, move forwards slowly everyone, left foot first, and don't forget that you four at the front need to thrust your swords out on the second count. Are you ready?'

They didn't look as if they were but there was a muffled cry of, 'Ready!' from inside the giant metal tortoise, so Mark began barking out the instructions.

'And one and thrust, and one and thrust, and one and thrust, and one and thrust.'

Becky watched as the assembled group began to inch forward towards her and she found herself edging backwards. It was an intimidating sight, and it really helped to give her an idea as to how the real Roman Army would have been able to use the formation with such devastating effect, until Johnno tripped over at the front, and they all came crashing down on top of each other amidst rattling, moaning and general armoured cursing. But she got the idea. They just needed a lot more people!

'When's your next event?' she asked Mark, who turned around and walked back to stand next to her.

As they both enjoyed watching their fellow Roman Imperialists disentangle themselves from each other, Mark replied, 'Well, the next main one is Bath's annual

Roman Day parade, in two weeks' time. It's not exactly a battle re-enactment, but more of a chance for us to show Bath what we're all about.'

'I didn't know Bath had a Roman Day parade!'

'It's never been huge, and hardly gets a mention in the press, but the local council has given us permission to march around town once a year carrying our swords and shields.'

'What, all nine of you?'

'Well, yes!'

'I really think we can do better than that.' She reached over and took hold of his hand. They both felt a rush of adrenaline with first contact.

'How about we go and pick up all that Roman equipment from the Basin Museum?' she suggested.

'Really? Well, yes, of course, that would be great, but wouldn't they mind?'

'They might mind a bit, so it would probably be better if we just don't tell them.'

They looked at each other and smiled.

'Another thing,' Becky added. 'We could really do with some more people. Why don't we think about organising some sort of a recruitment drive, in time for the parade?'

'Yes, but I'm not sure how. We've already stuck up a few posters around the university, and I did give out some leaflets at the Fresher's Fair. Battle re-enactment just isn't that popular anymore. Most people would rather play Call of Duty.'

'Posters and leaflets? Isn't that all a bit last century?'

'I don't know, is it?'

'Do you have a website?'

'Er, no.'

'Facebook?'
'Um.'
'Twitter?'
'Er.'
'Pinterest?'
'What's Pinterest?'
'You're kidding?'
'Um.'

'Good grief! Looks like we've got work to do. What we need is some sort of a decent PR campaign. Something to raise awareness, generate a little interest and pick up a few more recruits. Let me think about it for a while, but first things first, we need that Basin armoury!'

'Yes, but how are we going to get it?'

'Oh, I'm sure we can think of something.'

'Maybe I could, er, buy you a drink and, um, we could talk about it, together?' Mark asked, having a go at nonchalance, but failing miserably.

She stood in front of him, ran one hand through his hair and kissed him lightly on the lips.

'I thought you'd never ask! Tell you what, why don't we skip the drinks and just do it behind that tree?'

Not waiting for an answer she grabbed his hand again and pulled him over to an old Horse Chestnut tree that she'd been eyeing up ever since she'd arrived. The previous day's misadventures had left her feeling more horny than usual, and she'd never been very good at small-talk.

CHAPTER XI
PSIDIUM LEPORES
Invasive rabbits

THE FOLLOWING DAY, a slightly less grubby white van turned into York Street with Mark sitting bolt upright behind the wheel, Becky as relaxed as ever in the middle and Doughnut, chosen for his ability to carry a heavy load, on the far passenger side; but their own mothers wouldn't have recognised them.

After their Roman Imperialists' training the previous day, they'd successfully managed to gain entry into the university's chemistry labs where they'd lifted three complete sets of white hooded forensic suits, along with masks, blue shoe covers and some thin blue latex gloves. Fully adorned, they now looked like genetically engineered bunny rabbits with no ears and blue feet, and nothing at all like three acting members of the Roman Imperialists out for some early Sunday morning shopping.

They had made an effort to clean up the van, as best they could anyway, and it was only then that Becky had laid out her devious plan: to retrieve the entire stash of Roman armaments from the Basin Museum the very next day, all in one go, simply by pretending to be from the British Environmental Agency.

So, as they trundled down York Street, if anyone did happen to look at them twice all they'd see would be three pairs of eyes surrounded by whiteness. They'd even put on clear plastic lab glasses, just to make sure formal identification was an impossibility.

Up ahead they could see that the Basin Museum was still zoned off with reels of blue and white tape that had "POLICE LINE DO NOT CROSS" stamped all over it. On this fine sunny morning three days after Capstan's discovery of the dead security guard, there still lurked a police Transit van, right outside the entrance.

As they drew close, a forensic investigator, fully zipped up in his own white ensemble and wearing the exact same blue gloves and shoe covers, staggered out of the museum carrying a large black plastic crate that seemed to be crammed full of laboratory equipment.

They watched him stop briefly to stare at them before he continued over to the rear of the already opened Transit. He dropped the crate onto the van's floor and shoved it down into what appeared to be an otherwise empty loading area.

'Pull up behind them, but not too close,' instructed Becky, as best she could through her mask. 'We don't want them to see just what a pile of crap our van is!'

She then picked up a clip board from off the dashboard, along with her student union card that she'd brought along especially for the occasion.

'OK boys, out you hop, but let me do the talking - and remember, don't use your real names!'

With that, all three of them clambered out, rather awkwardly, and lolloped over to where the forensics man sat on the back of his own van to remove his shoe covers.

As they approached he took off his mask, pulled back his hood and then stood up to unzip his overalls.

'Who's in charge here?' Becky demanded with a tone that rang with authority.

The man pulled his white overalls over his shoulders and pushed them down his arms to his waist.

'I am! Why, who are you?'

Becky's protective glasses had already begun to steam up, so she gave up with both them and the mask, and took them off.

'My name's Professor Cathy Cakeburt. We're from the British Environmental Agency,' and she flashed her student union card at him as quickly as humanly possible before pinning it straight back inside her clip board. 'And you are?'

Impressed by both the credentials and the stunning good looks of the woman presenting them, the forensics man stuck his hand out.

'Batter, Paul Batter. I'm Head of Bath City Police Forensics Department.'

'Good, then you're just the man I need to talk to. We've been alerted to a dangerous chemical discharge that's been traced back to the Basin Museum and we'll need immediate access to investigate.'

'Crikey!' said Batter, even more impressed. 'I'd better take you straight in then. Hold on a mo.' He pushed his overalls all the way down to his feet, sat on the back of the van again to pull his legs out, and then stood up, leaving the overalls just lying on the pavement, to head straight back into the museum.

Becky smirked at both Mark and Doughnut and they all followed him inside.

Clearly delighted with the success of her initial subterfuge, Becky thought she may as well take the opportunity to find out how the police investigation was going, the one at the Basin Museum anyway. So as they entered into the dimly lit, charity shop-smelling lobby, she asked, 'So, what's been going on here then? Why all the police interest?'

'Oh, nothing much really. A body of a man was discovered a few days back. He'd fallen into one of the basins, but despite the fact that he had a Roman sword sticking out of him, and that someone had thrown a life-sized statue on top of him before submerging him under at least five tonnes of water, we haven't been able to conclusively prove that it was foul play. He may have died when he fell backwards into the basin, but equally he could have been killed by the sword. Saying that, it's possible that the statue might have finished him off, or that he drowned. Either way, we've been unable to establish an accurate cause of death or whether anyone may have deliberately lent a hand in his demise, so we've given up and have been ordered out.'

'Oh!' said Becky, relieved to discover that Bath City Police Forensics Department was equally as stupid as those leading the investigation, if not more so.

As they entered the museum's dark, damp corridor Becky could see five or six more overall-clad forensic scientists, all hopping about at the bottom of the four ancient Roman basins. Just then, Paul Batter stopped dead in his tracks and turned around to ask, 'What exactly are you looking for?'

Becky had been expecting that question at some point, and she was fully prepared for it.

'Groundwater contamination, usually caused by highly corrosive metal being stored at a low-lying level.

There must be a large amount of bronze, copper or iron that's been stacked up around here somewhere. All we need to do is find it and then remove it from the premises as quickly as possible.'

'Well, we've been here for three days now and haven't found any piles of metal anywhere. It must be coming from the Roman Baths next door.'

'Um…' Becky said, thoughtfully, and she nudged her way past Batter and pretended to have a good nose around whilst making her way down towards the end of the corridor, where the stone bench sat in front of the large purple curtain.

When she got there she turned back to ask, 'What's behind here?'

'I'm not sure that there is anything behind there. It's just a wall, isn't it?'

Becky stepped over the stone bench, grabbed hold of the heavy curtain and heaved it all the way back.

'Aha! And what do we have here then?'

There was an audible gasp from her small audience as the corridor extended by about ten feet to reveal two more Roman Basins; but these sparkled and shone like a couple of Aladdin's Caves, as each was stacked to the brim with a variety of shiny new-looking swords, spears, shields and armour.

'My God!' Paul exclaimed. 'Chaps, you'll never believe what the British Environmental Agency has just discovered. Quick, take a look!'

As fast as they could, all the giant police bunnies began to emerge from the depths of their temporary subterranean warrens to make their way over to where everyone else now stood, mouths open at the sight of this bounty of priceless Roman treasure.

'Right!' exclaimed Becky, not wishing to push her luck any more than she already had. 'We need to get this lot out of here as quickly as possible. Clearly it's all been stored here for quite some time and God knows how much of it has corroded.'

But now, as she looked over at the immense hoard, she realised that it was going to take the three of them an absolute age to carry it all out to the van. Ever resourceful, she turned to Paul, who was still just standing there staring at this newly discovered treasure trove, wondering why he hadn't thought to look behind the curtain himself, as it did seem like a rather obvious place to look, now that he thought about it.

'I don't suppose you and your team could give us a hand to take it all out to our van, could you?' she asked, glancing back at it all. 'There does seem to be rather a lot of it.'

Batter was now beginning to wonder just how much trouble he'd be in when his boss, the Chief Inspector, returned from his sailing holiday to hear that his Head of Forensics had neglected to look behind a rather large curtain during a three-day possible murder investigation. Coming to the conclusion that he'd be in a lot less trouble if there was nothing behind the curtain at all, apart from two more empty basins, he answered, 'Yes of course! Anything to help the British Environmental Agency.' Then he turned to look at his assembled staff of rabbits and said, 'Come on chaps, let's give them a hand.'

With that, Mark and Doughnut picked up the heavy stone bench and carried it out of the way, leaving everyone else to pile in to grab as much treasure as they could carry.

As Paul himself started to help he looked down and saw one unusually elaborate sword, with a stunning jewel encrusted hilt. He reached down and pulled it out. It was truly magnificent! Sensing a huge surge of power course through his veins, he raised it up to stare at it. Lost in the moment he was about to cry out, "By the Power of -!" but saved himself a lifetime of ridicule by simply asking, 'Where do you want it?'

'Back of the van please,' replied Becky.

She caught Mark's eye and asked, 'Can you open it up for them, and then hop inside to get it all stacked away?'

'No probs!' Mark replied, hiding a wide grin behind his mask and reaching down to grab a sword of his own, along with a shield, breast plate and a spear, before heading out to the van.

Doughnut also helped himself to an armful of treasure, as did the six other forensic scientists, and they all followed each other out.

About half an hour later, the back of Mark's van was fully loaded, right up to the roof. Mark slotted one more sword in, and Doughnut closed the doors and locked them before the whole lot could fall straight back out again. But they'd only managed to empty the first basin, and as the chain gang of workers came to a standstill, Paul could see their predicament.

'Would you like to borrow the police van?' he asked Becky. 'We've hardly started to load it up yet, and it's much bigger than this one.'

'Really?' she asked, with genuine incredulity. 'That would be fantastic!' and before he could change his mind said, 'Come on lads, let's get the rest loaded!'

After about another half an hour, Becky emerged from the museum carrying the very last of the armour. But as she approached the Bath City Police van she saw Jeffrey Hetheringshaw, the Basin Museum's Senior Curator, waddling up York Street towards them. She'd completely forgotten about him and mentally kicked herself for not realising that he was bound to show up, sooner or later. She realised that it would take him a while to make it all the way up to them, but one thing was certain: when he did get there he wasn't going to fall for her little environmental contamination ploy. In fact he'd probably have a massive heart attack the moment he discovered that his entire museum had been cleaned out.

She crammed the last of the treasure into the police van and, as Paul kindly closed its doors, said, 'Thanks, Paul, I can't tell you how much we appreciate your help, but we really need to get this lot back to the lab as quickly as possible to begin our tests. Is it OK if we drive your van to our lab and drop it back later, say in about an hour's time?'

'Yes of course, no problem at all.' He fished out the keys from his pocket and gave them to her. 'We've still got all our equipment to pack up and then we'll probably take lunch, so please, help yourself.'

'Thanks, Paul, I owe you one!' and she winked at him.

Paul blushed and looked awkwardly at the ground. Like most people he wasn't used to being winked at by anyone at all, but especially not by a devastatingly beautiful young professor.

Becky looked back over her shoulder just in time to see Jeffrey enter the museum. She estimated that they only had a couple of minutes before they'd be rumbled.

'Right boys,' she called out, 'I'll take the police van and Mark, you take yours and I'll meet you back at the Lab.'

'Right you are, Becky, I mean… er, Cathy, Professor, lady, person, girl.'

Mark had really put his foot in it and Becky darted a glance over at Paul to see if he'd picked up on it. Fortunately for all of them, Paul seemed to be lost in thought.

Anyway, they had no time to lose, so she made her way around to the police van's door, clambered in, started the engine and proceeded to do a quick three-point turn before heading down York Street.

Mark did the same in the other van, with Doughnut back in the passenger seat, and as they both drove past the museum's entrance they all waived at Paul and his forensics team, who'd gathered outside to see them off. And as they all waived back, Jeffrey Hetheringshaw came stumbling out of the museum, clutching at his chest. The game was finally up, but the deed was done, and now they just had to make it out of the city centre before Mark's van's rear axle broke under the weight of its unusually heavy load.

CHAPTER XII
PUTEUS, QUEM FUNNIEST RES
Well, it's the funniest thing

FORTY MINUTES LATER, it was Capstan's turn to drive down York Street towards what was now a brand new crime scene.

At first glance, as he approached the Basin Museum, all he could see was an ambulance and what appeared to be a large number of mutated rabbits herded around the museum's entrance, nibbling from a variety of lunch boxes. When he pulled up he could see that the giant bunnies were avidly watching a couple of paramedics prodding at the prostrate body of some poor elderly chap.

Turning off the engine he had to admit that he was hardly in the best of moods. Throughout the entire journey from his home to the museum, his mind had remained firmly with his wife, and what she was about to do to him, which she probably wouldn't be prepared to do again until the following Sunday, and then only if he was lucky. He did appreciate that occasionally being forced away from his family at the weekends was all part of the job, but he'd have been much happier if, on this particular occasion, the call could have come half an hour later. Habitually he enjoyed spending his Sunday mornings barricaded inside his bedroom with his wife, away from their children, where they enjoyed doing things to each other that they'd both generally regret afterwards.

Having driven down in his own car, after he'd left a message on Dewbush's answerphone to meet him at the museum, he'd just become acutely aware that he didn't have a siren, and so was unsure as to how best to announce his arrival. So, as he stepped out of the car and locked it he attempted to catch someone's eye, but everyone seemed to be so pre-occupied with whatever it was that they were doing, they didn't even notice he was there. The rabbits were too busy eating, the paramedics were too busy life-saving and the man lying on the pavement was too busy dying.

So Capstan decided to make his way into the museum's lobby, where he saw someone sitting behind the reception desk with his head buried deep in his hands, apparently staring at a notepad covered in financial calculations.

'Er, excuse me!'

The man looked up. He didn't look very well and the only response he seemed able to manage was to raise a single eyebrow.

'I'm Police Inspector Capstan.'

The man now looked even worse.

'I understand there's been an incident here,' Capstan continued, pulling out his identification.

Paul Batter had been expecting the police to show up, probably because he was the one who'd called them, just after Jeffrey had stumbled out of the museum crying, 'Robbery! Robbery! We've been robberied!' before collapsing on the pavement. It was only then that the penny dropped and he realised the terrible misjudgement he'd made. Not only had he done nothing to stop the three so-called British Environmental Agency officials from walking out with what, in hindsight, was nothing less than a huge haul of priceless treasure, but he'd actively helped in the process. He'd even taken the liberty of encouraging the entire Bath City Police Forensics Team to lend a hand.

But as he stared at this police inspector it dawned on him that he'd also offered the criminals use of his team's van, as both a heavy stolen-goods transportation vehicle and as a get-away car.

He'd not survive this one, not with the recent cut backs they'd been seeing; and since using the museum's phone to call his own police station to let them know of his predicament, he'd been sitting there, trying to work out if he had enough money tucked away for what was sure to be a forced early retirement. Having just calculated that he didn't, and so was doomed to spend the remainder of his days stacking shelves in his local supermarket, he'd become even more depressed. But he thought that he could at least go down with dignity. Maybe this new police inspector would be a gentle, understanding sort of a man who'd be easy on him? So he stood up, straightened his tie and introduced himself.

'Hello, I'm the Head of Bath City Police Forensics Department, Paul Batter. We haven't met before. I take it you're new here?'

'Relatively, I suppose,' replied Capstan, but he already felt like he'd lived there since the beginning of time, and wished he hadn't. 'So, what's been going on here then?'

Batter sighed and just thought it best if he told it straight, whilst leaving out as much detail as possible.

'Well, it's the funniest thing! These three people arrived a couple of hours ago who we all thought were from the British Environmental Agency. They said that there'd been some sort of a leak from the Basin Museum, so I showed them inside and that's when they found all this hidden Roman treasure! Then they carried it all out to their van and drove off.'

He ended his statement with a big smile, hoping that this new police inspector would be happy with that and just slope off quietly to file his report.

But Capstan didn't move and just stared at him, so Batter thought he'd better make it clear that he'd finished by adding, 'And that was that really!'

Capstan finally blinked and looked behind him, hoping that Dewbush had arrived with his notebook, but he hadn't.

Turning back to this rather sad-looking man, Capstan said, 'Right then!' and decided that he was going to have to make a start on this one without Dewbush's expert note-taking skills, and would just have to do his best to remember everything that was said.

'So, why did you think they were from the British Environmental Agency then?'

Batter sat back down again. He clearly wasn't going home any time soon, not that he'd ever thought he was.

'Well, because they arrived in a white van and were dressed up in overalls that were the same as ours really.'

'So, that meant that they were from the British Environmental Agency?'

'No, of course not, but the girl in charge said that's

where they were from and she did show me some identification.'

'And what did that say?'

'I can't say I looked at it too closely.'

Capstan wasn't surprised. Since starting his job he'd noticed that nobody had given his more than a courtesy glance.

'Did this girl say what her name was, by any chance?' he asked, with some hesitation, not sure if he really wanted to know.

'I think it was Professor Burnt Cake, or something like that. I really can't remember.'

'Can you describe her?'

'Well, I suppose you'd say that she was… attractive.'

'Attractive or very attractive?'

'To be honest I'd have to say that she was the most beautiful girl I'd ever seen in my entire life!'

With some reservation, Capstan asked, 'What colour was her hair?'

'I couldn't say, it was all tucked up inside her hood, but I could tell that there was a lot of it. I did notice that she had blue eyes and pale white skin and that her eyebrows were black. So, taking a guess, I'd say that she had dark brown or maybe even black hair.'

Becky bloody Philips! Capstan thought, and shuddered.

'So, what happened then?'

'Well, as I said, I showed them inside and they found the treasure. Then they just took off!'

'But didn't you do anything to stop them?'

'Well I, er, no. You see, we thought it was all contaminating the water table, or something, and they seemed to be very keen to remove it as quickly as possible.'

'No kidding?' asked Capstan, with more than a hint of sarcasm. He was just beginning to wonder if everyone in Bath was a complete muppet. 'Perhaps you could show me where they found the items that they took?'

'Yes, of course, through here.' Batter led Capstan out through the back of the lobby and down the murky corridor that lay between the four publically displayed basins.

When they arrived at the now half open curtain at the end, he pulled it back a little more and said, 'These two basins were hidden behind here.'

Capstan was as surprised as everyone else. He too had never thought to look behind the curtain, assuming that it was just used to cover up an otherwise blank and rather unattractive wall.

'Christ, I had no idea!'

'No, neither did I. I'm not sure anyone did, except for the curator outside.'

'So, what was in here then?'

'Oh, they were both full to the brim with swords, armour, shields, spears… that sort of thing.'

'There must have been a hell of lot of it. How did they get it all out?' he asked with genuine curiosity.

'Um, well, they carried it.'

'What, all of it?'

'Er, yes, sort of.'

'And you just watched them?'

'Well, no, we actually, er, did help them a little.'

'You helped them carry it out?'

'Um, yes.'

'So they had guns then?'

'Er, no, not that I saw.'

'Did they threaten you in some way?'

'Oh no!'

'Then why on Earth did you help them carry it out?'

'I'm not sure really. It just seemed to be the right thing to do.'

'So, giving three criminals a hand to remove what must have been tonnes of priceless Roman artefacts just seemed like the right thing to do?' asked Capstan, at a complete loss.

Batter didn't answer, but just looked down at his shoes.

'And how the hell did they manage to fit it all into the back of their van?'

'Um, well, we couldn't get it - sorry, I mean *they* couldn't get it all in, so they took our van as well.'

Rubbing his forehead aggressively with his hand, Capstan asked, 'So, you let them use your van to transport the stolen goods and as a get-away vehicle?'

'Er, I suppose so, yes.'

Feeling like his brain was being stretched like an elastic band on the end of a five year old's finger, Capstan had had enough.

'You're going to have to give a formal statement to my Sergeant. Where the hell is he?'

'Right here, Sir!'

Capstan nearly jumped out of his skin.

'Christ! For God's sake Dewbush, how long have you been standing there?'

Dewbush looked down at his notebook and said, 'Since that man there said, "SO THEY TOOK OUR VAN AS WELL"' in a loud, clear voice and with a devious smirk.

'Yes, thank you Dewbush, that's quite enough of that. Take down this man's statement and then meet me outside.'

'Yes, Sir, of course, Sir. Sorry, Sir!' replied Dewbush, still smiling.

Pushing past him, Capstan made his way back out into Bath's fresh, clean air where the mutated bunnies still stood and Jeffrey Hetheringshaw still lay, but now with a red blanket on top of him, a white pillow under his head and a stretcher laid out, ready to cart him off.

'Will he be alright?' he asked, as one of the paramedics passed by.

'It's difficult to tell. He is very old. At first we thought he'd had a heart attack, but he was breathing normally and his heart had a steady beat. He may have just fainted, but he could also be suffering from shock and he did hit his head quite badly when he keeled over, so we're not moving him until we've done a few more tests.'

'Do you think it would be OK if I asked him a couple of questions?'

'Well, you can try, but I don't think you'll get much sense out of him.'

Feeling like he'd been unable to get much sense out of anyone recently, he crept over and knelt down beside the old man. From this close up, he looked like he was completely dead. His skin was grey, his eyes were closed and he didn't seem to be breathing at all. Capstan placed a hand on his bony little shoulder, shook it a little and whispered, 'Mr Hetheringshaw? Mr Hetheringshaw, it's Police Inspector Capstan. Can you hear me?'

There were absolutely no signs of life and Capstan was about to call over the paramedics when, without warning, Jeffrey sat bolt upright, grabbed Capstan's lapels and screamed, 'SHE'LL KILL US ALL! SHE'LL KILL US ALL! THE SLAUGHTERED VIRGIN OF ZENOPOLIS WILL KILL US ALL!' directly at Capstan's face. Then, just as quickly as he'd sat up, he fell straight back down again, stone dead.

Having been trying to push himself away from the old man's clutches, Capstan now fell over backwards onto the pavement as the two paramedics launched themselves over to see what was going on.

'Bloody hell!' said one of them. 'That was a bit dramatic! What on Earth did you ask him?'

'Nothing! I didn't have a chance! He just grabbed me and started shouting!'

With a quick look they could tell that he'd probably passed on and so, with no further need for caution, the paramedic closest to Capstan said, 'Right, we need to get him to the hospital.' They then picked the old man up, dumped him on the stretcher and carried him off to the ambulance where they slid him inside. Then, as one stayed in the back with him, the other closed both rear doors and jogged around to the driver's side before setting off in a blaze of sirens and red flashing lights.

Dewbush emerged from the museum, just in time to see it head off. He'd heard Jeffrey's rather ominous prediction from all the way inside, and now seeing his boss still trying to pick himself up from the pavement, made his way over to give him a hand.

'Are you all right, Sir?'

Still in shock, Capstan gratefully accepted

Dewbush's help and slowly got to his feet. Once up, they both stared after the ambulance as it disappeared around the corner onto Terrace Walk.

'What was all that about?' Dewbush eventually asked.

'Frankly, Dewbush, I've got no bloody idea. He just grabbed me and started shouting. Something about that bloody statue!'

'The Slaughtered Virgin of Zenopolis. Yes, I heard.'

'Well, it scared the life out of me!'

'Is he...?'

'Dead? I bloody well hope so!'

'Blimey! His last words then?'

Capstan shuddered for the second time that day. He knew exactly what the old man had said to him, and wasn't sure if he'd ever be able to forget it. Then a small voice behind him piped up.

'Can I go home now please?'

It was Batter, hoping that this new distraction might help get him off the hook.

Turning around to face him, Capstan slowly remembered why he been called out to the museum in the first place and said, 'No, you bloody well can't go home!'

Then, looking around at the assembled forensic investigators, he continued, 'As far as I can make out, the lot of you are accomplices to grand theft, knowingly or otherwise, so you can all take yourselves down to the station and wait there to be questioned!'

They all looked at the pavement in shame.

'But Sir!' said Dewbush, 'Don't we need them to stay here, to start re-examining this new crime scene?'

Capstan gave out an audible sigh and looked up

towards heaven. Dewbush was right of course, but as Bath City Police Forensics Department couldn't even establish the exact cause of death of someone who'd obviously been stabbed with a Roman sword, he thought the chances of them finding any actual evidence of wrong doing, when they themselves had lent a hand in the crime, seemed all rather unlikely.

He rubbed his forehead vigorously with the palm of his hand again.

'Oh, very well.'

Looking back at his half-bunnified audience he said, 'Will you all please now treat this as a brand new crime scene and report back to me just as soon as you can?'

Then he looked at his Sergeant.

'Dewbush, stick around for a bit and take down their statements will you?'

'Yes, Sir, of course, Sir.'

'Then you may as well go home. We'll have to think up a new plan of action on Monday morning. I'm really not up for doing anything more today.'

Capstan ambled his way over to his car, staring down at the ground like a broken man. Once inside, he just sat there and gazed at the steering wheel for a while. He could hardly remember what all the major crimes were that had taken place over the last week, let alone solve any of them. So he thought he'd better do something to help collect his thoughts and dug around to find a half used family-sized box of tissues and a pen. On the back of the box he then scrawled out the following.

Bank Robbery: Suspects - Becky Philips + three other men! Proof – none!

Suspicious death of security guard: Murder? Accidental?

Suspects – Becky Philips?? Proof – none!

Basin Museum Robbery: Suspects – Becky Philips??? + 2 others. Proof – nothing yet!

Theft of Police Van: Suspects – as above. Proof – ?

Writing the list out only made him feel more depressed: four crimes, at least two of them major, possibly three if his boss logically deduced that a man wouldn't have stabbed himself with a sword and then jump backwards into a Roman Basin before asking someone to throw a statue on top of him and drown him under five tonnes of water.

He helped calm himself down by remembering that his boss was still going to be away for another two weeks, and that the press had only found out about the bank robbery, and that the theft of a million pounds hadn't been enough to make it of national importance. As long as nothing else happened between then and when the Chief Inspector returned, and as long as the press didn't find out about the museum theft, the police forensics team assisting in the robbery, the police van being used as a get-away vehicle, and the museum's curator dying right outside after predicting that the Slaughtered Virgin of Zenopolis would kill everyone on Planet Earth, he should be OK.

Then he saw something move in his rear view mirror.

'Bugger!' he said, quietly to himself. He turned around to make sure that what did look very much like a white van with a large satellite dish lumped on top of its roof, was in deed a white van with a large satellite dish lumped on top of its roof, and not a figment of his imagination; not that he had much of one, but he had rather hoped that this was a figment of it, and not, in fact, Bath's press descending down upon him.

For a brief moment he contemplated suicide. A Roman sword would do it. Maybe that's what happened to the security guard? A life spent walking up and down a dark, damp, charity shop-smelling museum became all too much for him, so he ran himself through with a sword he found lying about. But Capstan didn't have a sword, and he didn't keep a gun in his family car, so he resigned himself to the fact that suicide was just going to have to wait. Maybe he could persuade Dewbush to talk to the press for him, whilst he hid behind the reception desk, until they'd all gone away? But as Dewbush himself had only just managed to escape incarceration for being a pervert, he probably wasn't the best man for the job.

And so, with a deep hollow sigh, Capstan stepped out of the car to meet the press for the second time that week.

CHAPTER XIII
MANI CIS ET LOTIS MACHINAS
Handcuffs and washing machines

IT WAS THURSDAY afternoon, nearly two weeks after the Basin Museum had been cleaned out and, to Capstan's relief, absolutely nothing had happened since, nothing of a serious criminal nature anyway. Yes, a washing machine had been stolen from YouGet on Sunday afternoon, and a rather embarrassed young man had been discovered handcuffed and gagged, stark naked, to a lamppost on Monday morning, with a message scrawled over his torso in bright red lipstick announcing to the world that he was getting married in the morning, which he wasn't, as he'd been there since Saturday night; but apart from those two minor events, Bath's residents had managed to act in full accordance with the law, to the very best of Capstan's knowledge anyway.

So with all being quiet, Capstan had his feet up on his desk while he busied himself with a crossword, courtesy of the Daily Bath's brand new Puzzle Page, which they'd just started due to an ever-declining lack of advertisers and which had been skilfully compiled by their part-time receptionist.

'It sounds like rope and is what you use to wash?' he asked himself aloud, staring out at another blue-sky afternoon through his grubby little office window.

It was only the first question, one across, but he was already stumped, and a quick glance through the remaining twenty-three left him sighing with self-indignation. He'd never been good at them but always thought he should be. Having grown up watching Morse with his Mum, he considered that any detective worth his salt should excel at them, so he did his very best to keep practicing and was always careful to discard each failed attempt before anyone had the chance to discover his complete ineptitude for them.

There was a knock at the door.

'Come in!' he called out, delighted that someone was about to witness him undertaking such an academic pastime.

Dewbush pushed open the door. He also had a copy of that day's Daily Bath, but he carried his in front of him with both hands, like a school boy who'd been caught behind the bike sheds with a copy of Spank n' Wank, and his trousers down.

'Afternoon, Sir,' Dewbush said quietly, not sure if he'd just woken Capstan up from his normal lunchtime snooze. 'Have you seen today's Daily Bath?'

'Yes, of course I have.' he replied, tapping loudly on his copy with a biro. 'What about it?'

'It's Roman Day, Sir!'

'What, today?'

Capstan had no idea what Roman Day was, and certainly didn't have a clue when it should take place. However, given that he was currently in charge of law and order throughout the city, he thought he'd better make it appear that he did know what it was, whilst being careful to use the correct level of casual indifference suited to a man of his position.

'No, Sir, it's not until next weekend.'

'Oh yes, that's right.'

Tapping loudly on his newspaper again, Capstan continued to stare out of the window.

'It's on the front page, Sir,' continued Dewbush, hoping to engage a little more interest.

'Is it? I can't say I'd noticed.'

'Yes, Sir, and there's another piece about it inside.'

'I see!' said Capstan, wondering what Dewbush was driving at, but still focussed on what someone may use to wash themselves that rhymed with rope and had four letters. So he looked at "one down" and read the clue to himself.

'It sounds like tower and is what you might have instead of a bath?'

Capstan beamed with delight and wrote down, "s h o w e r". Then he tapped the paper again, deep in thought.

'Something you use to wash yourself that sounds like rope, has four letters and the first letter is an "S"?'

He heard Dewbush cough behind him, which broke his concentration.

'Just exactly what is it that you want, Dewbush?' he asked, pulling both feet off the desk to replace them with the paper, before swivelling around to look directly at his subordinate.

'I just thought you should know, Sir.'

'Know what? That it's Roman Day next week and that it's in the paper?'

'Er, yes, Sir.'

He was about to tell him to sod off back to wherever it was that he'd crawled out from and find someone else less important than himself to discuss the contents of that day's Daily Bath, but he refrained. He'd always known Dewbush to exemplify the phrase, "Young, dumb and full of cum", especially after his recent clandestine wank-fest, but he'd never known him to be quite so obtuse. Furthermore, Dewbush had never shown an interest in the news before, local or otherwise, so Capstan had to consider the possibility that maybe he was trying to tell him something important, that perhaps had been mentioned in a recent memo, or that concerned a case that he was supposed to be working on but had forgotten about.

Now realising that he'd never bothered to read a single message that had passed his desk, electronic or otherwise, since he'd started the job, and that there'd been numerous cases which he'd never considered worthy of his time, like the washing machine theft or the naked man chained to the lamppost, he asked, 'Remind me Dewbush, just exactly what does happen on Roman Day?'

'Oh, it's Bath's annual Roman parade, Sir. It's when a few people get dressed up and march through town for an hour or two.'

Still none the wiser, Capstan probed further. 'Yes, and...?'

'Well Sir, it's normally a very low-key affair that tends to go unnoticed, so we've never bothered to cover it; just ten or so people wondering around carrying a couple of swords.'

'I still don't see your point, Dewbush. Are you asking for time off to go?'

'No, not at all, Sir, but it does seem to be getting rather a lot of press recently.'

Dewbush then opened up his copy of the Bath

Daily and placed it down on Capstan's desk before stepping back to give his boss an unobstructed view.

The headline, laid out in the usual panic-inducing black letters, factually stated, "BATH BRACES ITSELF FOR ROMAN INVASION".

Now that did catch Capstan's eye.

Somewhat surprised he'd not noticed it when he'd picked it up from the local newsagents', he sat up and read the first paragraph out loud.

'Bath's Annual Roman Day Parade takes place next Saturday. This year more than two dozen people are expected to take to the streets, fully dressed up in Roman armour, and all carrying real-life swords and shields.'

By the time he'd reached the end his voice had become monosyllabically flat, like a manic depressive reciting his own suicide note before jumping off a nearby cliff.

Unable to hide his disappointment - that there clearly wasn't going to be a Roman Invasion after all - he pushed the paper away from him and glowered up at Dewbush.

'You can go now,' he said.

'But, Sir?'

'No, I'm sorry Dewbush, but I fail to see how a few people's decision to wear some rather out-dated clothes can possibly be seen as a threat to the local population.'

'Well, no, Sir, but I've never known it to be mentioned in the press before and I just thought that in light of the recent events at the Basin Museum, with all those swords and armour being stolen, it may be wise for us to keep an eye on it, Sir.'

At last Capstan had managed to put the two

together.

'Yes, I see what you mean,' he said, still not wholly convinced that a couple of dozen people dressed up as Roman soldiers could cause civil unrest, with or without some stolen swords. However, with everything that had taken place the previous week, and with his boss having emailed him the day before to say that he'd extended his holiday due to a volcano erupting in Mongolia, Dewbush was probably right and it would be wise to take some precautions, no matter how benign the whole event sounded.

'Oh, very well! Have a word with the Duty Sergeant and tell him that we'll need a few hands to cover this Roman Day thing.'

'Yes, Sir. Right away, Sir.'

As an afterthought, Capstan asked, 'I don't suppose you have any idea how many men we do have on hand at the moment?'

Over the last couple of weeks he'd become acutely aware of the distinct lack of police personnel hanging around the station, which was one of the many reasons why he was keen for nothing more dramatic than washing machine theft to take place, at least not until his boss returned.

'Not many, Sir. Most are still away. Probably around ten.'

'Well, if nothing else important comes up between now and then, we may as well have them all on duty that day. Whilst you're here, Dewbush, I don't suppose there's been any more news on the Basin Museum case?'

'Which one, Sir?'

Capstan's eyes narrowed as he looked up at him.

Dewbush did have a point, there had been a number of un-solved cases relating to the Basin Museum, but he'd obviously meant the theft of the Roman armoury and thought Dewbush should have been able to deduce that.

'You remember… last Sunday… Basin Museum… Roman Armour… ring any bells?'

'Yes, Sir, sorry, Sir. Unfortunately not, Sir.'

'How about the bank robbery then?'

'Again, no, nothing.'

'Oh well,' and with that, Capstan's mind fell back to thinking about something less stressful.

'Before you go, I don't suppose you know the answer to one across?' and he looked over at the Puzzle Page to read out, '"Sounds like rope and is what you use to wash." It has four letters and the first one is an S?'

'Could it be "Soap", Sir?'

'Yes, I think it is!' exclaimed Capstan with delight, closely followed by heated resentment. It was a very obvious answer after all, and the fact that he'd just managed to show himself to be a complete tool by asking someone as low ranking as Dewbush was an uncomfortable feeling. However, it was hardly the first time, so he followed it up by saying what he always did in such circumstances. 'That's exactly what I thought it was! Thank you, Dewbush. You can go now.'

Suppressing a smirk, Dewbush exited the meeting with, 'Thank you, Sir.' and disappeared out through the door and headed off to find the Duty Sergeant.

CHAPTER XIV
OBTINUIT EAM
Got it

AT AROUND the same time, Becky was in Bristol with Mark, sitting outside a café on Hannover Quay and staring out over the River Avon. Despite looking very much like your average couple skiving off work on a Thursday afternoon, they were there on business, which was why Becky had her eyes glued to a brand new pair of binoculars that she'd picked up from YouGet, in Bath, the Sunday before.

By chance she'd actually seen the washing machine theft take place, the one that Capstan had already filed as "unsolved". A heavy-set man in his early thirties had entered the store shortly after she'd popped in. After selecting and paying for a large kitchen knife, he'd lined up to pick up his item from their You've-Almost-Got-It Point B, in a similar way to most people shopping there. However, as soon as it had been given to him, he'd used it to threaten various members of staff before staggering out with a brand new washer-dryer.

Being abundantly aware of the many suspicions already stacked up against her, Becky had decided to stay out of the affair for a change. She was even reluctant to hold the door open for the man as he'd weaved his way out. And as soon as he'd left, she'd rejoined her queue, desperate to pick up her order before Capstan arrived. Fortunately for her, the store's staff had been thoroughly trained for such acts of criminal desperation, certainly more so than those at the Instathon Bank, and were able to carry on with their work as if nothing much had happened. Subsequently, by the time Capstan did show up, she was long gone.

And so, with her new binoculars buried deep inside one of her more generous handbags, along with a beach towel, some sun cream and the normal paraphernalia that accompanied her wherever she happened to go, she'd driven with Mark up to Bristol earlier that day, where they now sat, preparing to undertake a rather daring PR initiative that, they hoped, would also drum up a few more recruits for the Roman Imperialists.

'Can you see anything?' asked Mark, trying to stay awake.

Having spent the last two weeks on a "sight-shagging" trip around Bath with his new all-too-promiscuous girlfriend, he was exhausted.

'Not much,' Becky replied, with her normal abundance of energy. 'I think there are a few people at the back, near the helicopter, and maybe some more at the top, where those big windows are. It's difficult to tell, really.'

With the glasses still held firmly against her eyes, she was scanning the length and breadth of a long grey battleship that lay moored up on the far side of the river. It was HMS Britannica, a Type 82 Destroyer that formed part of the Royal Navy's surface fleet.

Like most modern day battleships, the Britannica was a sight to behold. At just over five hundred feet long and with a displacement of six thousand, four hundred tonnes, she dominated the view from the café, and just about everywhere else in Bristol. She'd been commissioned by the Royal Navy in 1982, just in time for the start of the Falklands War, but had broken down half way there and had to be towed back. Being unable to effect the necessary repairs in time, she'd missed the war and spent the next twenty five years endlessly circumnavigating the British Isles, looking for something to use as target practice that nobody would miss too much.

Several thousand nautical miles later, and an unknown number of missing Norwegian fishing boats, she'd sprung a leak. But the engineers were unable to locate the source and moored her up in Bristol Harbour to continue their investigations.

Eight years on, they were still looking; and so there she remained, no more to roam the great oceans of the world but still able to provide cheap accommodation for over two thousand Royal Navy personnel, most of whom were male and all of whom had nothing to do all day except check the ship's coordinates and practise tying a few knots.

After a couple more minutes of intense observation, and with her eyes and arms feeling the strain, Becky handed the glasses over to Mark.

'I guess they must all be below deck,' he eventually said, with some apprehension as to whether there was anyone on board at all.

Becky looked at her watch, finished the remnants of her coffee and said, with a mischievous smile, 'Right, I'd better be off then!'

'Are you sure about this?' asked Mark, with some concern.

She stood up, turned to place her handbag on the chair she'd just vacated, and started rummaging around inside it for her towel and sun cream.

'Don't worry, I'll be fine.'

She leaned over, gave him a quick kiss and said, 'Look after my bag,' before striding off, like an erotic pendulum, down to the quayside's edge.

Directly ahead of her lay Sally Anne, a sparkling white, 62 foot CloudCatcher motor yacht that they'd watched moor up alongside them about half an hour before. Five minutes after that, they'd seen it being gaily abandoned by its middle-aged crew who, as far as Becky could overhear, had decided that they desperately needed to buy something, but couldn't quite decide what.

When she reached the foot of the boat's galvanised steel gangplank, she paused. She knew this was going to be her most ambitious undertaking to date and, although still confident the plan would work, was very much aware of the risks involved. Glancing over both shoulders she took a deep breath and set off up to board the glamorous, if not rather ostentatious, vessel.

On reaching the top, she took hold of the starboard side railing and inched her way along the narrow walkway, one foot in front of the other, towards the bow. Once there, she let go of the railing and stepped onto the yacht's opulent teak foredeck before taking in the view. Confident that the location would suit her needs to a tee, she pulled out the towel from under her arm and laid it out over the decking. She took a quick look over her shoulder to make sure Mark was still there, guarding her handbag, and then, without further hesitation, dropped her sun cream down onto the towel, slipped off her sandals, wriggled out of her tight white shorts, pulled off her t-shirt, unclipped her bra, and slowly smoothed her pants down to her feet before stepping out of them and kicking them to one side. Completely naked, she then crouched down to retrieve the sun lotion and stood up again to begin massaging the rich, creamy fluid all over the many and varied undulations that made up her curvaceous young body. Satisfied that she'd reached every crack and crevice, she then laid herself out on the towel, facing up towards the cloudless blue sky.

She had about twenty minutes to kill, so with nothing much else to do, she closed her eyes and reflected on the many events that had taken place during the last few weeks, from the moment the dead security guard had been discovered, to when she'd met Mark and his little battle re-enactment group, and their daring raid on the Basin Museum.

With her demonstrable gift for leadership, she'd now been elected the official leader of the Roman Imperialists, and had embraced the role with a surprising amount of enthusiasm. Even before she was unanimously voted in, she'd already laid out a plan to make this the year they'd become a force to be reckoned with; and it would all start on Roman Day!

Thanks to the Basin Museum they had enough uniforms, shields and swords to weaponize a small army, all piled up, ready for action, in the university's chemistry labs, which were still vacant due to the long summer holidays. They'd also found themselves in possession of a police van, which was nice, but they weren't sure they'd need it again, so Becky had driven it back to the police station and left it in their car park, thinking that that would probably be the last placed they'd think to look. Sensibly, however, she'd kept the keys, just in case they needed it again.

Over the course of a ten day period she'd also managed to persuade Mark to phone up the Daily Bath, in an effort to drum up some publicity. Initially he was far from keen. He'd never been good at that sort of thing, as he'd shown at the bank, but after resorting to the use of an elastic band and a pencil, that made a highly effective little tourniquet, Becky had been able to change his mind. So he'd called them up to remind them about the forthcoming Roman Day, which they'd completely forgotten about. After chatting with them for half an hour, he'd given them the front page story and the feature article that Dewbush had just brought in for Capstan's unrequited attention.

But she knew it wouldn't be enough. The Daily Bath was hardly the Sunday Times, and for her elaborate plans to come to fruition they were going to need a significant amount more publicity and a hell of a lot more recruits!

And so it was, that with those two objectives held firmly in her mind, she continued to lie, stark naked, on top of a luxury yacht in the middle of Bristol Harbour, hoping that at least one person on board HMS Britannica would be able to spot her.

CHAPTER XV
CLOUD VIGILANTES
Cloud Watching

CAPTAIN BLANKARD surveyed the view from HMS Britannica's Command Bridge as he'd been doing almost continuously ever since he'd first taken command of her some eight years before. He let out an audible sigh. Like the entire crew, he was completely bored. He'd done his Advanced Knotmanship course many years before, and subsequently had nothing to do all day except to check the ship's coordinates and stare out of the window, praying to God that North Korea might invade, or maybe America, as they were closer.

He lifted his Royal Navy issue binoculars to take a look at Bristol Harbour's podgy little ferry, as it plodded its way over to the far bank. He'd watched it make the same journey at least a dozen times already that day, maybe more, but he really didn't have anything else to look at. He had recently developed an interest in nephology, the study of clouds, and did enjoy looking at their unusual formations; but as it was a blue sky day, he was left with little choice but to watch the ferry make the same journey, over and over again.

When it reached the other side of the river he trained his glasses along the harbour's far side quay, to see if there were any civilians worth looking at, but there were hardly any around. Then he stopped.

'Now, what do we have here?' he asked, loudly, hoping to engage the attention of his subordinate officers.

Not surprisingly they all looked up; after all, it was rare for them to hear the voice of their Captain. He normally spent the day just sighing, loudly, so this sudden multi-syllabic vocalisation made them all stop their coordinate checking activity in the hope that he might be calling their attention to something interesting for a change. The last time he had made such an audible remark was when he'd spotted a cloud that looked like Marilyn Monroe, but it really didn't, and they'd all returned to their posts nurturing a growing feeling of resentment towards him and his new hobby.

But in desperate need of a distraction, the ship's most junior officer, Lieutenant Haffinger, asked, 'What is it, Captain?' Quite frankly, he didn't care if it was a cloud that looked like Santa's beard. He'd been at his post since seven o'clock that morning, endlessly checking the ship's exact same coordinates, and had, just moments before, been contemplating suicide, or a job in sales.

'There's a girl… on the far side bank, walking over that CloudCatcher yacht.'

By the time Blankard had finished the sentence, all four officers had retrieved their own Royal Navy issue binoculars and had lined up alongside him.

Silence fell as they observed a stunningly attractive woman with lashings of dark brown hair and the smallest, tightest white shorts ever conceived by mankind, stepping onto the yacht's foredeck to lay out a large, purple towel. With mouths hanging open, they continued to watch as she began to undress, until the moment she reached behind her back to unclasp her bra.

'My God!' exclaimed Blankard. He couldn't believe his luck. Neither could his fellow officers. But when she started to peel off her pants as well, Blankard knew exactly what he had to do.

With each passing year he'd been forced to observe the morale of his ship descend to ever depressing depths. As far as he could fathom, the only benefit HMS Britannica had was towards Bristol's many and varied employment agencies, not the Royal Navy. Recruitment firms throughout the West of England had seen their profits increase exponentially, year-on-year, since the mighty ship had arrived, and Bristol had become one of the few places in the United Kingdom where a Junior Recruitment Consultant could place an able and willing candidate into a normally impossible-to-fill position, like a Telesales Executive or a Trainee Letting Agent, within ten minutes of receiving the job spec. And despite working hard with his officers to come up with some exciting new ideas to keep the crew occupied, like the poorly received "Ship's Coordinate Checker of the Year Award", which nearly started a riot, or the ill-fated "24 Hour Knot-a-thon", that proved too much for some who'd used their ropes to hang themselves, most days Blankard felt lucky if everyone simply made it out of bed in time for lunch. On average he lost a quarter of his crew each year, to either the local job market or the Grim Reaper, but at the end of the day, it really didn't matter. Each time he lost someone, the Royal Navy would send him a replacement, so he never felt short-staffed, just terminally bored. He also found himself feeling permanently guilty. He believed that it was his duty, as Captain of the ship, to provide his crew with a rich and rewarding environment for them to work in, but he'd found the task almost impossible.

So, as soon as the girl had kicked her pants away, he forced himself over to the ship's main intercom where he lent forward, pressed the small red button, and said, with his normal quite reserve, 'Code Six, starboard bow.' He then stood up to re-take his position at the viewing window, re-focused his binoculars and continued his surveillance whilst listening to his own voice reverberate around the ship.

Within moments, all the officers noticed something, and it had nothing to do with the girl they'd been staring at. The Britannica had begun to heel, ever so slightly, over to starboard. Then they heard a noise more associated with a sinking submarine. Without question, the vessel had started to go over!

Blankard realised his error. The term "Code Six" was the unofficial way to advise Royal Navy personnel of a stunningly attractive woman, but he'd never used it before, not on the Britannica anyway, and certainly not over the ship's main intercom. In his desperation to spread the good news he'd forgotten that the vessel had only been designed for a crew of three hundred and ninety-seven, but now it accommodated over two thousand men, all of who were now falling over themselves in a bid to secure a prime viewing position on the starboard side of the boat. He'd possibly just made the single biggest mistake of his naval career.

As the ship continued to list, all the officers exchanged rather concerned looks, and each instinctively placed one hand on the rail in front of them. Then they just stared out with a sense of inevitability, as the River Avon began to creep ever-closer towards them. Just as Blankard was about to give the order to abandon ship, the groaning and creaking subsided and the vessel came to a halt, levelling off at what was just a rather unusual angle.

'Should I record the ship's new position, Captain?' asked Haffinger.

He'd never known it to have moved before, and was keen to make a note of it.

The girl had just picked up her sun lotion.

'Um, hold that thought for now Lieutenant. Let's just, er… continue to make our coastal observations for a moment or two, shall we?'

So they renewed their vigil, just in time to see the girl start to apply the sun cream to her arms.

A couple of minutes later she'd made her way to her breasts and the ship started to hum with a curious, muted vibration. It was almost as if a single engine had been started up, but Blankard knew that was impossible as they'd broken down years ago. He didn't realise that it was the sound made by two thousand male crew members, all masturbating together as one, as they sated themselves after months of pent-up sexual frustration.

It wasn't long before the girl finally put the sun cream away and, for all those below decks, disappeared from view as she laid herself out on the towel.

With their hedonistic pleasure now over, the crew slunk back to whatever it was that they'd been attempting to occupy themselves with before, a little disappointed that their free entertainment had finished so quickly, but also buoyed by the prospect that there could be a "second coming"; and with that in mind, each cabin had appointed someone to act as lookout.

As his ship return to a more appropriate angle, Captain Blankard also decided to leave someone on watch before excusing himself. He was in desperate need of providing relief to his own intimate frustrations, as well as a drink, and thanks to his right hand and a hip flask, he was able to do both, pretty much at the same time, and in the privacy of the Bridge's en suite toilet.

CHAPTER XVI
CORRUERE, SIVE NON CADERE
To fall or not to fall

BECKY WOKE UP. It was hardly the plan to fall asleep on the job, but was probably the result of the many attentions she'd been bestowing on Mark over the last couple of weeks. She looked at her brand new waterproof watch - bought from YouGet, along with the binoculars - and sat up. She'd already been there half an hour and had carelessly slipped behind her own self-imposed schedule.

She yawned, stretched herself out and gazed over towards HMS Britannica, which looked exactly the same as it did before. Standing up, she glanced over towards where Mark had been. He was still there, along with her bag, but his head now hung down on his chest. Assuming he hadn't been assassinated by a rival battle re-enactment group, or had had a heart attack as a delayed reaction to their recent over-exertions, and that he'd simply fallen asleep, she looked down at herself to see if she'd been able to catch any sun. There did seem to be a vague white mark under each of her soft, heavy breasts and so, satisfied that she was just a little browner than before, she picked up her t-shirt, pulled it down over her head, retrieved the towel from off the decking and headed over to the boat's port side railing, to stare again at the battleship. Then, using one hand to hold on to the railing and the other her towel, she carefully stepped over the rail and sat on it, enjoying the coolness of the chrome against her warm, bare bottom. With both feet now resting on the gunwale, one hand still on the railing, and the towel under her arm, she leaned out to look down over the boat's side. It was probably about a ten foot drop to the water below. She shrugged. Then, hooking her feet around the rail's base stanchions, she took the towel out from under her arm and, with both hands now free, found its two adjacent corners and gave it a half-hearted shake. Confident that she wasn't going to lose her balance she shook it again, but this time with a little more vigour. A sudden gust of wind sprang up from nowhere, caught the towel and plucked it from her hands. Without thinking, she reached out to grab it but immediately slipped off the rail and plunged into the water below, giving out a girlish squeak on the way down. Then she vanished beneath the cool, murky waters of the River Avon, leaving behind just a few ripples to radiate outwards until, they too, disappeared from view.

CHAPTER XVII
OMNES MANUS DISSOLVENTUR UNIVERSAE MANUS
All hands, all hands

'HAVE I MISSED anything?' asked Captain Blankard as he emerged from the head, still buckling his belt.

'No, nothing, Captain. She's still just lying there,' reported Haffinger, who was relishing his new position as lookout. 'She hasn't budged an inch.'

'Very well. Keep your eyes peeled and let me know if…'

'Hold on, Captain, she's moving.'

Blankard was about to hit the ship's intercom again to announce this latest development, but remembering what happened last time he thought better of it. So instead, he simply picked up his binoculars and headed over to the window to take a look for himself.

'She's sitting up, Captain,' continued Haffinger, unable to hide his excitement. 'And now she's standing!'

The remaining three officers hurried over to join their Captain and junior Lieutenant, and were now all peering out through their binoculars in silent adoration. Haffinger, however, was so absorbed by his new role that he didn't notice any of them line up alongside him, and so continued with his running commentary.

'She's putting on her t-shirt.'

They all watched as she squeezed herself into it. Then, as she made her way towards the CloudCatcher's port-side, Haffinger announced, 'She's moving towards us!'

As she lifted one of her legs to step over the railing he cried out, 'She's still got no pants on!'

All five pairs of binoculars began to tremble slightly, but remained held firmly against their eyes.

The commentary soon continued.

'I think… yes, she's going to shake her towel out. Yes, she's shaking her towel! She's shaking her towel!'

This powerful movement made her breasts undulate in such a way that even the most stubborn case of erectile dysfunction would have been cured.

'She's going to shake it again! Yes, but, no… it's gone! The towel's gone. The wind must have… SHE'S GONE! SHE'S GONE IN, OVER THE SIDE!'

Without a moment's hesitation, Blankard launched himself over to the command console and hit the general alarm button. As the giant vessel sent out a deafening wail over the harbour, he stumbled towards the main intercom.

'THIS IS CAPTAIN BLANKARD. ALL HANDS! ALL HANDS! THERE IS A WOMAN IN THE WATER, STARBOARD BOW! THERE IS A WOMAN IN THE WATER, STARBOARD BOW! ALL HANDS! ALL HANDS! LAUNCH IMMEDIATE RESCUE! I REPEAT, LAUNCH IMMEDIATE RESCUE!'

General panic swept the ship.

First to react were the Britannica's three powerboat crews, who'd all been watching from the same shared cabin. Having been fully trained for such emergencies they knew instinctively what to do and raced each other out to the sea-level quarter deck, where their black ribs lay waiting like ominous shadows against the ship's light grey hull.

Not far behind, and unwilling to be left out, came the rest of the two-thousand strong crew who'd all, just moments before, been hanging themselves out of every porthole along the entire length of the ship's starboard side. Within a minute of the alarm going off they spewed out onto the deck, like a tidal wave of genetically engineered sperm, each one carrying an object they'd picked up along the way, thinking that they'd make better impromptu rescue volunteers if they brought with them something that could float. And as soon as they'd reached the battleship's railings they jettisoned whatever it was that they'd brought with them and then simply followed on after, plunging down into the harbour below.

Sadly, it was only then that most of them realised two things. Firstly, that although objects like holdalls, paper-back books, potted plants, porn mags, the box they were kept in, two tins of baked beans, a toasted cheese sandwich and a broken toilet seat did indeed float, unfortunately they all seemed to lose their innate gift for buoyancy when descended upon from a height of thirty feet up; and secondly, that only a few of them could actually swim. The Royal Navy had never considered swimming to be a necessary requirement for a life at sea, as anyone going overboard normally did it wearing a life jacket, and only then when the ship was sinking, which was a rare event, even during the darkest times.

The ship's officers, those who weren't on the bridge, watched helplessly as the vast majority of their crew began to drown, and moments later launched their own rescue mission, to save as many of them as possible, and before they reached the point of becoming dangerously under-staffed.

But now, as a barrage of hard polystyrene flotation rings and huge white boxes containing automatically inflating twenty-four man life rafts began to rain down on those now desperate to keep their heads above water, those who were about to drown did, and those fairing a little better found that having to dodge a variety of missiles being aimed directly at their heads was a bridge too far, and so, they too, started to go under.

Seeing their shipmates in trouble, the few who could swim made a gallant effort to disperse the flotation rings out to as many people as possible, and as soon as the life rafts had inflated, the vast majority of men were at last able to find something substantial to cling on to.

Then, when most had stopped coughing up water, they put the unfortunate incident behind them and, en masse, started paddling out over the river to continue their rather ill-advised rescue mission.

Blissfully unaware of what his crew was going through, Captain Blankard and his fellow officers continued to scan the water where the girl had last been seen.

'Can anyone see her?' he asked for the second time, unable to hide his growing anxiety.

They were all waving their binoculars around as if attending a bird-watching convention in Florida during the hurricane season, as they desperately searched for any signs of movement.

With rising desperation Blankard asked again.

'FOR CHRIST SAKE, CAN ANYONE SEE HER?'

'No, nothing, Captain!' Lieutenant Haffinger answered, trying not to cry. 'She's just… vanished!'

'Shit!' said Blankard.

Desperate to do something to help the poor girl, he hit the intercom again.

'THIS IS CAPTAIN BLANKARD TO THE HELICOPTOR RESCUE CREW. THERE IS A WOMAN MISSING IN THE WATER, FAR BANK, STARBOARD BOW. IMMEDIATE SEARCH AND RESCUE IS REQUIRED.'

He took his finger off the intercom and checked the nearest radar monitor before re-pressing the button and continuing, 'THE AIR SPACE IS NOW CLEAR. YOU HAVE MY PERMISSION TO TAKE OFF!'

Just moments later the Britannica's resident Helicopter Rescue Crew emerged from below decks and scrambled over towards the ship's large red and grey Sea King Mk5. It was, as always, fuelled and ready to go, so the pilot, co-pilot and airborne rescue team all climbed aboard to start making their way through the various pre-flight checks just as quickly as formalities would allow. It wasn't long before the engine started to whine and the blades began to rotate, and as the noise intensified the ten-tonne monster lifted into the air, rotated around, dipped its nose forward and then thundered off towards the far side bank.

CHAPTER XVIII
NON SUM MORTUUS
I'm not dead

UNUSUALLY FOR BECKY, before falling overboard she'd had second thoughts. Approaching the rail she'd seen no more movement on HMS Britannica than she had when sitting outside the café with Mark. Yes, it did seem to be lying at rather an odd angle, but apart from that it looked very much like it did before, meaning that her intended plunge into the harbour would not only be a complete waste of time but quite possibly rather dangerous as well. She was a strong swimmer, or so she thought, but had no idea how fast the current was and if she'd simply end up being swept off downstream to be run over by a passing container ship in the Bristol Channel.

The towel had made up her mind for her. She honestly hadn't expected it to take off like that and considered it to be a good omen. But as soon as she'd gone in, and then under, she knew she was in trouble. She'd expected to float straight back up again but there was a powerful undertow which was pulling her down, and keeping her there.

She panicked, kicked out and clawed her way back up.

Breaking the surface she took an almighty breath, choked, and breathed in again. Then she twisted around in circles, desperate to find something to hold on to and cursing herself for thinking that she was a good swimmer. The last time she'd done something that could be described as swimming had been in a Spanish pool whilst on holiday with her Mum and Dad about ten years earlier.

Then she heard the wail of what sounded like an air-raid siren.

Just my luck, she thought, *to jump off a boat the moment China decides to launch a nuclear air strike.*

Trying not to let herself be side-tracked by the possibility of being left to drown as the rest of the world rushed down to Safebusy's for some last minute panic-buying, she peered over towards the Britannica and was mortified to see that it must have already been hit by something. Her view wasn't great but it looked like the entire crew had started to abandon ship by throwing themselves overboard, along with everything else. Her concern for the crew, and civilisation as a whole, rose significantly when she saw numerous orange life rafts burst into life all around the ship, and then watched aghast as hundreds, possibly even thousands of people, attempted to swim over towards them.

Then the giant helicopter that she'd observed earlier lifted off the ship, hovered for a moment and then ploughed off towards Hannover Quay. On the off-chance that they might be kind enough to pick her up on the way, she attempted to wave at them, but they paid her no attention and just continued to fly over the river. As far as she could make out, they were heading to where she'd been just five minutes earlier, but she wasn't there now! The current had already taken her a fair way from where she'd fallen in, and it was doing so at an alarming rate.

Increasingly concerned for her immediate future she started shouting, screaming and waving as best she could without allowing herself to go under again. Thankfully, one of the pilots must have seen her as it rotated around and began heading straight for her.

As well as the Sea King, three powerboats that she hadn't even noticed before all turned sideways as they came off their high-speed planes to drift up towards her.

'ARE YOU OK?' bellowed out a voice from the nearest boat.

With the helicopter fast approaching, and with the noise it was making along with everything else, she could only just hear what he'd asked. Her first thought was that it was a bloody stupid question, given the circumstances, and was about to shout back that she wasn't dead, if that's what he meant, when she was hit by the wake from the powerboats and her head submerged back under the surface again. So, when it bobbed back up, all she could manage was to shout, 'YES!' whilst nodding vigorously.

'WE'RE GOING TO HOIST YOU UP INTO THE HELICOPTER!' the man shouted back.

The Sea King was now directly overhead and blasted air down at her with a disconcerting force. Becky owned the most powerful hairdryer on the market, the Nuke Zone Atomic 5000, and subsequently thought her head would survive a German car manufacturer's wind tunnel; but this was something else entirely.

The powerboat driver closest to her manoeuvred his rib away and then gave a thumbs-up signal to the helicopter above. Through her hair and the huge amount of spray, she could barely see anything at all and could only just make out someone being lowered down towards her, but she was tiring fast and could feel herself beginning to slip under again.

Everything went quiet.

Someone jumped in beside her and pulled her back to the surface where they were joined by the man who'd finished his descent. Both men then worked together to secure her into a harness before clipping that to the end of the helicopter's cable. Another thumbs-up was given, and the line tightened before Becky was slowly hoisted up into the air and to safety.

And as she rose out of the water, the two thousand men who'd all been paddling like demented river race competitors, arrived at the rescue zone just in time to gaze up in wonderment at Becky's wet, perfectly formed naked bum. And as soon as she'd disappeared from view, and the helicopter had started to thunder back towards the ship, they all splashed along after it, just as fast as their over-crowded orange life rafts could go, hoping to make it back in time to personally welcome her on board and ask for her phone number.

CHAPTER XIX
BEATUS BATH DAY
Happy Bath Day

IT WASN'T LONG before the Sea King landed back on board HMS Britannica and Becky, now wrapped up in an emergency foil blanket, was helped down on to the ship's deck.

Directly ahead of her was an official welcoming party, all breathing hard as they stood to attention. The group was made up of those wearing Royal Navy officer's uniforms and those in black wetsuits who each stood in his own puddle. The officers were a combination of the men from the Bridge, who'd raced each other down as soon as they'd seen the helicopter return, and the men from the deck, who'd helped prevent the entire crew from drowning - well, most of them anyway. Those wearing the black wetsuits were the powerboat crews, who'd only just made it back in time.

When Becky looked up at them they all saluted in unison, and as they did, the two men who'd winched her to safety escorted her over.

As she approached, Captain Blankard stepped forward. He gave her another quick salute and then said, 'Welcome aboard HMS Britannica, I'm Captain Blankard. We're all exceptionally pleased to have you safely on board!'

With the formalities now over, he stopped saluting and asked, with genuine concern, 'Are you alright

Miss, er...?'

'Becky! Yes, Captain, I'm OK, and thank you. I can't say how stupid I feel, and how sorry to have put you all too so much trouble.'

'It really was no trouble at all. Our only concern was for your safety. Now please, come inside and warm yourself up. You must be freezing!'

Mindful of her mission she replied, 'I really am fine, thank you. I could probably do with a shower but I don't suppose someone could wash my t-shirt for me? I only picked it up from the printers yesterday, and I'd hate for it to be ruined.'

With that, she unwrapped herself from the foil blanket and pulled her dripping wet t-shirt all the way down to her still naked thighs, to show her assembled audience.

They all stared down at it and started to read, with ever-widening eyes.

BATH'S ROMAN DAY
SAT, 29ᵀᴴ AUG, FROM 10AM
Parade Gardens, Bath
Roman Army March - led by Rebecca of Bath
Lavish Roman Feast
Bath's Bonkettes - Adult Entertainment
FOOD, DRINK & WEAPONS PROVIDED
REGISTER ONLINE
www.RomanDay.co.uk

Captain Blankard looked back up at her as if she was an angel sent down from heaven itself carrying many tidings of great joy. Roman Day sounded like his best day out ever and he knew that it would be the perfect antidote for his bored, unmotivated and near suicidal crew.

He gave her a broad smile.

'That looks absolutely splendid!' Then, out of simple curiosity, he asked, 'Who is Rebecca of Bath?'

'Oh, that's me!' and she returned her own sweet, home-baked smile to him. 'Just a bit of fun really.'

Standing near the back with his hand up, Lieutenant Haffinger called out, 'Miss, Miss, can I take your picture?'

'Not now Haffinger, for God's sake!'

'Oh, I don't mind at all,' she purred. 'It really is the least I can do. Tell you what, how about one with all you boys standing behind me?'

Haffinger pushed his way forward and started acting as an impromptu studio director.

'OK everyone, move in please. C'mon, push right in. That's it! Now, Miss, can you come forward a bit, and maybe face towards me a little?'

As everyone grouped in behind her, all grinning like demented garden gnomes, Becky positioned herself to face Haffinger whilst attempting to do something with her hair. Then she stretched her t-shirt down to her thighs again, looked at it and then back up at the camera.

'Like this?' she asked, attempting to look like the picture of innocence, but failing on all counts.

'Oh yes! That's just perfect! Right, everyone ready? OK, smile! That's great, now, just a few more.'

'Come on, really!' interrupted Blankard, 'I think that's quite enough pictures for now, thank you Haffinger.'

'I really don't mind Captain,' Becky said, adding,

'Maybe it would be better if I just took my t-shirt off?'

And before anyone had a chance to say another word, she'd done exactly that, and began posing all over again, but now wearing nothing at all.

Haffinger cleared his throat and started taking just as many pictures as he could before either he, or the curvaceous sex goddess that undulated in front of his eyes, was arrested.

Fearing that he may be about to lose control of both himself and his ship, Blankard brought the whole thing to an end.

'Now that really is quite enough of all that!' he said, and picked up the foil blanket to give to Becky who, begrudgingly, wrapped herself back up in it.

'Well, alright.' she said, handing her t-shirt to him. 'But can you please wash that for me? It really is very precious.'

'Yes, of course! Now please, Miss, er, Rebecca, won't you step this way. I'll show you to my cabin where you can have a nice hot bath, in private.'

As he led her away he started chatting to her, enjoying the company of someone who wasn't either a Royal Navy Officer, or a man.

'I had the bath installed last year, you know. It's actually only the second one in the whole ship. And whilst you're getting yourself warmed up, we'll wash your t-shirt for you. Would you like any food? Something to drink maybe? We have a fine selection of…'

Haffinger and the remaining members of the welcoming party watched their Captain disappear into the ship with their new found pin-up, and just as soon as the iron door had been pulled closed, he turned to face them.

'What a girl!' he said, and then held up her t-shirt in triumph.

Everyone cheered and began crowding around to take a closer look.

Now desperate to tell all his friends, Haffinger scrolled through the various pictures he'd taken, chose the very first one and touched, "Send to Facebook". Just before posting it he wrote, "Look what we fished out of the harbour today!" but then had a stroke of genius, deleted that and instead keyed in, "Happy Bath Day everyone!" and hit the "share" button.

Then they all started taking pictures of themselves with the t-shirt, and it wasn't too long before the not-so official rescue party, all two thousand of them, had clawed their way back on board to join in with what was fast turning out to be the Social Media event of the decade.

But of all the pictures taken that afternoon, the one that captured the moment beyond all others was that of Becky, in her transparent white t-shirt, and her entourage of new found admirers. And as Becky soaked herself in Captain Blankard's steaming hot bath, the photo that became known as "Happy Bath Day!" spread around the globe to be viewed, liked, commented on and shared out by just about every male Facebook, Twitter and Pinterest user on this planet we call Earth.

CHAPTER XX
STILETTOS, SIZE QUINQUE
Stilettos, size five

BECKY GAZED UP at the ceiling from inside what was now a rather lukewarm bath, feeling very pleased with herself. The PR campaign had all gone according to plan - well, apart from the bit when she'd nearly drowned of course, but even that had taught her a valuable lesson: that she wasn't a strong swimmer after all, and the next time she decided to accidently fall off the end of a boat in order to attract the attention of a nearby battleship, she'd bring along some armbands. In fact, she'd also pack a rubber ring, some goggles, a snorkel and an industrial strength shower cap.

She lifted her hands to examine them. They'd most definitely "prunified". It was time to get out.

Heaving herself up into a sitting position, she reached for the plug's chain and pulled it out, stood up and stepped onto the bath mat, taking a fluffy white towel from the rail to dry herself.

Making her way into the main cabin, she wrapped the same towel around her head and, feeling self-indulgent, stopped to admire herself in the cabin's full length mirror. She'd never thought about it before, but she did look a little like that statue, the one of the Slaughtered Virgin of Zenopolis, back at the Basin

Museum. It was probably because she had such pale skin, with no obvious tan lines.

Just for fun, she adopted the exact same pose as that of the Slaughtered Virgin.

The likeness was uncanny, and it really spooked her.

With hairs standing up on her arms she shivered, and pulled the towel off her head. Then she remembered.

'Mark!'

She hadn't spoken to him since the café, and that must have been hours ago.

There was a knock at the door.

Wrapping the towel around her like a sarong, she headed over to open it.

There stood Captain Blankard, with a folded garment resting in his hands.

'I'm returning your t-shirt to you, as promised, Miss, er, Rebecca.' He was about to add that at least half the crew had tried it on before it was cleaned, but thought better of it.

'Thank you, Captain. That really is very kind of you.'

She took it off him and held it up to the light. It was immaculately clean but at least twice its original size. However, it had served its purpose, so she discarded it over her shoulder and changed the subject.

'I don't suppose you've got a phone I can borrow? I really must call my boyfriend. He must be worried sick!'

'Oh, yes, of course. Here, you can use mine.'

He took out his iPhone and gave it to her. Then he pulled himself up into a more formal stance and asked,

'Would you care to join us for dinner this evening? I don't know if you're free or not, but the officers would be delighted if you could dine with us.'

'That's very kind of you. Yes, I'd love to. Thank you!'

'And we have some members of the, er, local press who've come on board, asking for an interview. Do you think that would be alright, at some stage?'

'Well, I guess so,' she answered, pulling down a mangled clump of hair to examine it. 'But I can't possibly see them looking like this! I don't suppose there's any makeup on board, and maybe a hairdryer?'

'I'm sure we must have something somewhere,' Blankard answered, wondering if they still had any women left on board the ship at all. Then, as an afterthought, he added, 'And some clothes, perhaps?'

'Yes, I suppose so. Jeans would do, and maybe some stilettoes? I'm a size five.'

Blankard searched his pockets for a pen. His memory had never been good at the best of times; which reminded him.

'Oh, by the way, we also have Admiralty flying up from Portsmouth. They seem to be very keen to meet you as well!'

'Really?'

She was rather taken-aback. Her little stunt may have been more successful than she'd first thought.

'Yes, well, news does seem to travel fast these days.' A look of uneasiness swept over his face. He'd no idea how the British Admiralty had found out about it so quickly, and was more than a little concerned with what they'd have to say about the whole thing, especially in relation to the missing crew members.

'Meanwhile,' he said, turning his mind back to more pleasant matters, 'may I have someone come down to give you a guided tour of the ship? You can then help yourself to whatever you like from the canteen, and it will give the crew a chance to meet you.'

'Oh yes, I'd like that, very much!'

'Right then!'

He wasn't sure what to say next.

'I suppose I'll go and see about that, er, hairdryer and, um, oh yes, the jeans.'

'And the makeup,' Becky prompted.

'Yes, the makeup.'

'And the shoes. Please don't forget the shoes! Stilettoes, size five.'

'Of course, yes. Stilettoes, size five.'

'Thank you again, Captain. I'd really appreciate that,' and as he disappeared off down the corridor, desperately trying to remember all the items she'd asked for, Becky closed the door.

It was all going far better than she'd expected.

Looking down at the phone she tapped in Mark's number. He must know what had happened: by the sounds of it, half of England must have heard about it, but she felt a sudden urge to speak to him, just to make sure that he knew she was OK.

After chatting to Mark for around twenty minutes, there was another knock at the door.

'I've got to go. If you could pick me up at eleven, that would be great. Yes, thanks. See you then!'

She hung up and went to answer the summons.

'Good afternoon, Miss.'

It was Lieutenant Haffinger, holding a shopping

bag, and his nerve. He'd been desperate to meet her again, ever since taking her photograph.

'The Captain asked me to bring these down for you.'

'Oh, thank you very much!' she said, peeking inside the bag. 'And you are?'

'Lieutenant Haffinger, Miss. I was the one who took your picture, when you first came on board.'

'Ah yes, I remember.'

'He's also asked if you'd like a tour of the ship. The canteen's just down the corridor, so we could stop there first.'

'Yes, of course, I'd like that. Let me just get changed into this lot. Give me ten minutes.' She took the bag off him and headed back into the bathroom, leaving Haffinger standing outside the door, not sure what else to do as he hadn't been invited in, or told to go away.

Half an hour later, with Haffinger still standing in the corridor, Becky re-appeared looking flustered but in much better form.

'I'm nearly ready, hold on!' and she gave her hair a final prod in the mirror. 'There!'

Haffinger then proceeded to lead her down the corridor towards the canteen, where two thousand crew members had crammed themselves in, right up to the ceiling, all eagerly awaiting her arrival.

CHAPTER XXI
TERRAM RULES
Ground rules

THREE GLASSES OF champagne, a bottle of wine, numerous vodka shots and what she hoped had been the ship's "own brew", and not untreated urine, later, Becky edged her way down the HMS Britannica's gangplank, keeping her eyes firmly fixed on the narrow steel walkway beneath.

Ahead of her she could just about make Mark out, on the quay side below, propped up on the bonnet of her little yellow Mini Cooper, but she didn't dare wave at him, just in case she lost her balance, which wouldn't have been difficult.

When she did finally step onto the hard, she turned to look back up at the ship.

Captain Blankard, Lieutenant Haffinger and the two-thousand other crew members were still there waving, cheering and howling, like the cast from Twilight, Breaking Dawn, Part Four, The Musical.

Joining in with this rather boisterous send-off was the British Admiralty, as well as The Bristol Beagle's news team and every member of staff from the Daily Bath, who'd made it just in time to consume the last ten bottles of champagne.

Someone screamed down, 'WE LOVE YOU REBECCA!'

She beamed and bellowed back, 'I LOVE YOU TOO!' and blew them a kiss that would have intoxicated a thousand ships, but which spun her off to collapse against a nearby bollard.

More cheers and wolf-whistles followed as Mark came to her rescue.

'C'mon Becky, I think it's time we got you home.'

''ello, darlin', fancy meeting you here!' Then looking back to the ship, she called out, 'I'M GOING HOME NOW. BYE, EVERYONE!'

The catcalls changed to disgruntled boos, as Mark guided her away towards the car and folded her into the passenger seat. He made his way around to the other side, closed his door, and looked down at her with a certain amount of apprehension.

'How've u bin, my lover?' she asked him, in a thick West Country accent, before breaking down into fits of giggles for no apparent reason.

He rolled his eyes and then set off towards the A4 and the forty minute journey back home, all the while contemplating exactly what she'd been up to. At some point he was going to have to have a very serious talk with her. If their relationship was going to last more than a month, they'd have to lay down some basic ground rules; the first being that she wasn't allowed to gang-bang the entire crew of a Royal Navy Destroyer, even if it was in the name of the Roman Imperialists, and in return, he'd try to remember to put the toilet seat down.

CHAPTER XXII
FRONTE PAGE VIVAMUS SCELERISQUE
The front page headline

AT EXACTLY nine a.m. the very next day, Dewbush burst into Capstan's office, without knocking.

'Sir, Sir, it's Becky Philips, Sir!'

'For Christ's sake, Dewbush, I've only just hung my bloody coat up!'

'Sorry, Sir.' he said, stopping rather abruptly to lean on his knees and catch his breath. He'd run all the way from the car park and had forgotten just how unfit he'd become since joining the Force.

'Well, what is it then? I haven't got all bloody day!'

'Sorry, Sir.' he said again, 'It's Becky Philips, Sir. She's in the Daily Bath!'

Still with one hand on his knee, he waved the local newspaper for his boss to look at.

Capstan hadn't picked up a copy that morning. Having only been able to answer two of the clues from the previous day's crossword – soap, one across, and shower, one down - he thought he'd give it a miss for a while. He was also disappointed with their last front page headline, the one that suggested Bath was about to be invaded by a Roman army, which he found to be wholly misleading. So, with due caution, he removed the newspaper from Dewbush's hand, and sat down at his desk to take a look for himself.

'It's the front page, Sir. Look! It's her! Becky Philips! Right there, on the front page!'

'Yes, Dewbush, thank you. I can see it. Now, shut up, will you, and let me read the damned thing.'

'Yes, Sir. Sorry, Sir.'

And with that, Capstan started to ogle Becky's picture, in much the same way as most men had done around the world, all those living in a similar time zone at least. Then he started to read the article out loud, beginning with the headline.

'BATH GIRL RESCUED, BRISTOL FASHION.'

He looked up at Dewbush, raised an eyebrow and continued to read.

'A dramatic rescue took place in Bristol Harbour yesterday when student Rebecca Philips of Bath was heroically saved from drowning by the crew of HMS Britannica.'

Capstan looked up again at Dewbush, raised the same eyebrow, and carried on again.

'The ship's Captain, William Blankard, OBE, who was making coastal observations at the time, saw Rebecca fall off a nearby yacht and disappear. Taking immediate action, he sent out his entire crew to perform a massive search and rescue operation. Fortunately Rebecca is a fit, strong swimmer, so despite the harbour's dangerous under-tow, she was able to reach the surface and stay afloat long enough to be rescued. When interviewed, Rebecca said, "I don't know what happened! One minute I was sunbathing, naked, and the next thing I knew I'd fallen overboard; and if it wasn't for Captain Blankard here, and his amazing crew, I'd have been washed straight out into the Bristol Channel."'

Capstan turned the page over to find that the story continued on the inside, accompanied by various pictures, all of people drinking, dancing and rolling around on the floor.

He didn't bother to read the rest, closed it up and pushed it away from him. Then he sat back in this chair, put his elbows on the armrests and entwined his fingers together.

Silence followed as Capstan reflected on the article.

Dewbush, meanwhile, used the time wisely by gawping at the photograph. Eventually he noticed what she was wearing.

'Sir!' he said, picking up the paper. 'Excuse me Sir, but did you see what it says on her t-shirt?'

'I don't give a fuck what it says on her bloody t-shirt, thank you Dewbush.'

A muted silenced returned to the room, during which time Dewbush replaced the paper back onto Capstan's desk and decided to join his boss in deep, meditative thought, by folding his arms together and rubbing his chin a bit. But it wasn't helping him to come up with any insightful ideas about anything at all, so he just shoved his hands into his pockets and asked, 'What do you think she was doing, Sir?'

'Isn't it obvious?' Capstan asked, staring at him.

Apart from thinking that she may have been taking part in a Royal Navy wet t-shirt competition, Dewbush hadn't a clue.

Capstan continued to stare at him.

'Do you really not see what she was up to?'

He was tempted to offer up the wet t-shirt competition theory, but didn't want to risk it, so he just shrugged.

'She was trying to leave the country, you moron!'

'What, by going for a swim in Bristol Harbour?'

'Yes, exactly!'

'But… Where to?'

'Ireland, probably. Or maybe France.'

'France, Sir?'

'Yes, France! You know, it's that large country, next door to ours, where everyone speaks French!'

'Yes, I know France, Sir, but isn't that quite a long way for someone to swim, from the Bristol Channel?'

'Well, maybe, but it says right there that she's a strong swimmer, and she's most definitely fit, there's no question about that!'

Capstan looked at the picture again.

'She's probably spent weeks training for this.'

'Yes, of course, Sir.'

'But one thing it does prove, beyond all reasonable doubt,' he continued, 'is that she's as guilty as hell, and I was right all along.'

'Yes, Sir!'

Now that Capstan had suggested that she was trying to flee the country, it did seem rather obvious after all, and Dewbush kicked himself for not having thought of it first.

'So, what's the next step, Sir?'

'To arrest her of course, you incompetent fuck-wit!'

Dewbush was used to having derogatory remarks levelled against him, pretty much all of the time, but he'd never been called an incompetent fuck-wit before.

Capstan continued.

'Right, first we need to alert the relevant authorities to the fact that there's a suspected bank robber trying to make a run for it.'

'You mean a swim for it, don't you, Sir?'

'Shut up Dewbush! Now, she's probably trying to head for Ireland, but she could also be thinking of France. Tell you what, scan the entire front page and email it out to every port in the UK, including airports.'

'What about the Channel Tunnel, Sir?'

'What about it?'

'Shall I send it to them as well?'

'Yes, of course, send it to them as well! Why the hell wouldn't you?'

'Well, Sir, it's neither a port nor an airport. It's more of a... tunnel, Sir.'

Capstan could feel himself spinning out of control, which he demonstrated by snarling at his half-brained Sergeant.

'I'll just go and send this out to everyone then, Sir,' said Dewbush, edging himself away from his boss who glared at him like a cocaine-fuelled rhinoceros. And to Dewbush's relief, Capstan's door was still open, so he was able to continue backwards, grabbing the handle on the way and pulling it closed as he left.

Alone once more, Capstan turned back to stare at his barren, empty desk and said, 'Fuck-wit!' again, in an attempt to calm himself down. Then he got up from his chair and started pacing around the room, all the while thinking about Becky Philips and the various methods she might use in an effort to try and escape what was looking to be a considerable amount of time at Her Majesty's pleasure.

CHAPTER XXIII
MARCELLUS CONSILIO ADUOCATO
Council of War

THE FOLLOWING MORNING, Becky sat at her kitchen table, cradling her head in her hands. Directly in front of her was a large mug of coffee that Mark had just made, and just beyond that were all his student friends, otherwise known as the Roman Imperialists.

She'd arranged the meeting several days before, to discuss a final plan of action for Roman Day, but she'd been so pre-occupied with the planning and execution of her little PR stunt that it had completely slipped her mind. Had she remembered, she'd have postponed it for at least a day, but when she'd pushed Mark out of bed to answer the front door to be greeted by Doughnut, Sebastian and Johnno, she'd felt it was too late to cancel.

Mark started tapping on his mug of coffee with a tea spoon.

'OK, everyone, thanks for coming over.'

He was at Becky's right hand, with a laptop and that day's issue of the Daily Bath, both of which rested on a large map detailing the City of Bath which covered most of the table.

'We just thought it best to meet up again, to run through our plans for Roman Day, and to sort out any outstanding issues.'

'How was Bristol?' asked Doughnut, who, like everyone else in planetary orbit around the sun, already had some idea.

'Very successful, thank you,' and Mark picked up the newspaper and laid it out on the table for everyone to see.'

They all leaned in to take a closer look.

There, covering half the front page, was the now famous "Happy Bath Day" picture, and splayed out in giant bold letters underneath was written, "BATH GIRL RESCUED, BRISTOL FASHION".

'As you can see,' he continued, 'everything went according to plan and, as a result, we're expecting to have gained a few more recruits.'

Silence fell over the room as they all continued to ogle the picture. They'd seen it several times before, on Facebook, Twitter and Pinterest, but not on the front page of the Daily Bath.

Becky glanced at it. She had to admit that she did look good, considering the state her hair had been in, but was more interested to see whether the wording on her t-shirt could easily be read, which it could.

She turned to Mark.

'How many have signed up so far?'

'Oh, hold on. Er, let me see. Yes, here it is. Two thousand, one hundred and fifty four.'

'TWO THOUSAND, ONE HUNDRED AND FIFTY FOUR!' repeated Doughnut, with complete incomprehension. 'TWO THOUSAND, ONE HUNDRED AND FIFTY FOUR?' he said again, just in case nobody had heard him the first time.

'Yes, Doughnut,' said Becky, 'thank you, but you

don't have to keep saying it over and over.'

'But… how can we have two thousand, one hundred and fifty four? The last time I looked we had seven!'

'Well,' Mark stepped in, 'as I said, our trip to Bristol was rather successful and as a result we seem to have picked up a few more recruits.'

'Yes, but TWO THOUSAND, ONE HUNDRED AND FIFTY FOUR?'

'Fifty five now.'

'What?' asked Doughnut.

'Two thousand, one hundred and fifty five.'

Mark had refreshed the screen.

'And now fifty six.'

Doughnut shook his head.

'Yes, alright, I get it, but what did you do to get us up to two thousand and… however many?'

'Look, it really doesn't matter,' Becky said, keen to move things along. 'What's important now is that we have a plan in place to cope with them all.'

'No kidding!' said Doughnut.

He'd previously been in charge of marketing, and was feeling just a little put out by her rather sudden and dramatic success.

'Right, first things first,' Becky continued, pleased to be leaving the subject. 'Sebastian, how many swords, spears and shields do we have?'

'Oh, that's me,' said Sebastian, putting on his reading glasses. 'Right, we've got one thousand, three hundred and fifty seven swords, seven hundred and ninety two spears, and just over four hundred shields.'

'And armour?'

'Oh, I haven't counted that up yet, but I'd estimate

that it's about five hundred breast plates and around the same number of Centurions' helmets.'

'Well, it's not going to be enough,' said Becky, looking despondent.

'Can't we just buy some more from somewhere?' asked Mark. 'I mean, it's not as if we're strapped for cash!'

'We've tried that already,' said Doughnut. 'Which is why we lifted that lot from the Basin Museum.'

'You know YouGet?' Johnno asked, somewhat out of the blue.

'Yes, Johnno, I think we all know YouGet,' replied Doughnut, rolling his eyes.

'Well, my Mum told me that they've started selling party costumes, for adults, and that they had some Roman stuff in there.'

'Mark, look that up,' said Becky. 'If they have, then it's going to be our best shot for making up the shortfall. At least then, everyone will have something appropriate to wear.'

'OK, hold on. Yes, they do! Plastic though.'

'Doesn't matter. Do they come with swords and shields?' she asked, with renewed enthusiasm.

'Yes, both. Not bad considering, and just under twenty pounds each. Here, what do you think?' and he rotated the laptop around for her and everyone else to see.

'That will do!' she said. 'Just order two thousand of them.'

'Hold on,' said Doughnut, still feeling miffed at being made to look like he hadn't been doing his job properly for the last five years. 'If we buy all that stuff, then the new recruits will look the same as us.'

'Yes.' said Becky. 'I thought that was the idea, isn't it?'

'I know, but it's just not fair! We've been Roman Imperialists for years now. I don't know about you lot, but I've spent months practising all my battle moves. We can't just have two thousand newbies rock up and instantly become Roman Imperialists. They should look... different, somehow.'

Everyone murmured in agreement.

Becky sighed.

'Well, what do you have in mind?'

'Can't we do something to identify them as being new, like... I don't know, paint something on them?'

'How about sticking L Plates on them?' Mark suggested, surprised at his creative genius.

Becky looked around at him.

'Seriously?' she asked.

'Sure, why not? We can buy a couple of thousand L plate stickers and just slap them on their shields.'

'Sounds good to me,' said Doughnut.

Becky thought it was the dumbest thing she'd ever heard in her entire life, but was just too hungover to argue.

'OK, hands up, who thinks we should put L Plates on all the new recruits?'

Everyone raised their arms.

'Fine!'

Democracy really wasn't her thing, and she made a mental note not to make it an option in the future.

'Mark, can you look to see if YouGet sells them as well? We may as well order everything from the same place.'

'Yes, already checked. They do!'

'OK. Order two thousand of them.'

'Better make that three thousand,' added Doughnut, 'just in case some more people turn up on the day.'

'No!' stated Becky, putting her thumping headache to one side in order to retake control. 'That would mean ordering another thousand Centurions' costumes, and we're not doing that on the off-chance that a few more people show up.'

'Well, yes, but…' She could almost hear Doughnut's brain turning over as he tried to come up with a decent counter-argument. 'If more people do show up, and they also want to be Centurions, then we can just stick L plates on their heads. Then they'll know that they're members of the Roman Imperialists, but just haven't got their armour yet.'

Becky was staring at her coffee again.

Mark piped up.

'Tell you what. How about we order two thousand green P plates, for all those with armour, and a thousand red L plates, for those without?'

'The whole thing is getting far too complicated,' Becky said, losing her patience. 'Listen, Mark, just order two thousand red L plates, and if anyone else shows up, they can just follow along behind as… slaves or something.'

An excited commotion broke out as everyone discussed how cool it would be to have a bunch of slaves follow them around all day.

'Right, so, two thousand red L plates then?' asked Mark, looking around for approval.

'Looks like it,' said Doughnut.

'OK, I've added them to the shopping cart. Do we

need anything else from YouGet?'

Having now had time to imagine what two thousand people would look like, all marching through The City of Bath, dressed up as Roman Centurions with L Plates stuck to their shields, or heads, Becky was having second thoughts, but it was too late now.

'Tunics!' she said. 'We'll need a lot more. And leather belts as well.'

'Yes, OK, I'll add two thousand beige beach towels to the list, and the same number of belts. Anything else?'

'Food!' she said, feeling hungry.

'Anything else from YouGet? They don't sell food.'

'Oh, no, nothing that I can think of, but don't buy that lot yet. Something may come up later. Now, how much food are we going to order? Johnno?'

Johnno looked up with a start. 'Oh, er, yes, sorry. My Mum says that she can get Safebusy's to make a delivery for us next week, but we haven't actually placed the order yet. We were thinking of getting about twenty hamburgers, the same amount of baps, and about eighty cans of Bath's Best.'

'OK, good. When you do place the order, just add two zeros to the end of everything.'

'Okey-dokey, no problemo.'

'An email's come in, marked for your attention Becky,' Mark said. 'It's from a Lord Reginald Anthem. Well, his secretary anyway.'

Becky couldn't recall the name, but her memory from the previous night was a little hazy.

'What does it say?'

'That he's just making final plans to come over for Roman Day next weekend, along with his three

Spanish Stallions and two gold-plated chariots.'

A stunned silence fell over the room as everyone stared over at Rebecca.

'And he wants to know where he can unload them,' Mark finished off, before he also turned to face her.

'Oh, um...' She honestly had no recollection of talking to anyone about either horses or chariots.

Mark, keen not to dwell too much on the comings and goings of the previous evening, suggested, 'Shall I just tell him that they can be unloaded on Pierrepont Street, above The Parade Gardens?'

'Yes, thank you, Mark,' replied Becky, grateful that her new boyfriend didn't seem to be the jealous type. 'Now, I also think we need to provide some sort of temporary accommodation for our guests. They obviously can't all fit in here, it's only got three bedrooms, and they'll need somewhere to get changed as well. So I'd like to suggest that we buy some large marquee tents and put them up in the recreational grounds, opposite Parade Gardens.'

'The land on the other side of the river?' asked Johnno.

'Yes, that's right.' She pushed herself up to look down at the map. 'If we set up the registration desks here, in Parade Gardens, we can then funnel everyone over to our Base Camp, via Parade Bridge, here. That will give us all the space we need to collect people together, ready to start the march.'

Everyone seemed happy with the idea, so she said to Mark, 'Can you go to the YouGet site again and order twenty of their largest marquees?'

'Yes, no problem.'

'How about the route?' asked Doughnut, beginning

to warm to their new leader.

'Mark, can you answer that one for me?'

'Yes, of course.'

Mark was their new Chief Planning Officer, so he stood up and positioned himself over the map.

'Starting here, at the recreational grounds, I thought we'd cross the bridge, here, march into York Street, here, and then wonder around town for a bit.'

'I see,' said Becky, expecting him to have come up with something just a little more detailed. 'Is that what you did last year?'

'Yes, pretty much.'

She was disappointed, but too hungover to offer a more elaborate alternative, so she simply suggested, 'And then back to the base camp for the BBQ?'

'Yes, good idea!'

Now, desperate to get the meeting over with, she asked, 'Is everyone happy?'

Johnno put up his hand.

'Can we pop in to see my Mum?'

'When?' asked Becky, confused.

'On the way around. She's invited us all for tea.'

'Does she know that there's going to be about two thousand of us?'

'Well, no, but I'm sure she'd like to see us anyway. Couldn't we just go past her house?'

Becky sighed. 'Where does she live?'

'On Shaftesbury Road.' He leant over the map and pointed out its position. It was a small, residential street, about half a mile out of town.

Becky really didn't care.

'Mark, please make a note to head up that way at some point.'

'Yes, no problem.' He knew exactly where it was.

'Right!' she continued. 'If those horses and chariots show up, along with Lord… whatever his name was…'

'Reginald Anthem,' prompted Mark.

'Yes, him; then it looks like I'll lead the procession on one of the horses, leaving Mark and Doughnut to take the first chariot and Lord Anthem the second, assuming that's what he has in mind. Then everyone else can just fall in behind.

'Can you ride?' asked Mark. He hadn't a clue about horses, and doubted if any of his friends had either.

'Yes, I did dressage at school. Anything else?'

Sebastian put up his hand.

'Has anyone mentioned any of this to the local council, or the police? I'm sure it was fine when it was just the nine of us, but now, well…'

Becky was surprised nobody had brought this up before.

'Don't worry. I have a special relationship with Bath City Police. It won't be a problem,' and she waited for anyone else to raise a concern about it.

Nobody did.

'Right, does anyone else have any more questions?'

Again, there was silence.

'Great, well thanks for coming everyone, and I look forward to seeing you all in Parade Gardens, next Saturday, at ten a.m.'

Excited chatter broke out and Mark got up to join in.

Becky eased herself back into her chair and sipped at her coffee, relieved to have made it through. She then spent the next few minutes reflecting on the new information she'd been given; namely that, if she was now to spend the day on the back of a horse, she'd need something more appropriate to wear, other than the full body armour that had already been put aside. So she reached over and pulled Mark's laptop towards her, to take a look to see if Brides & Bondage had a sale on.

CHAPTER XXIV
DIE ROMAM
Roman Day

INSPECTOR CAPSTAN stood with his hands resting on the old stone balustrade that runs along Pierrepont Street, overlooking Parade Gardens.

'There's another coach arriving now, Sir,' said Dewbush, standing beside him.

They both turned to watch it pull up and bounce to a halt.

'And another,' Dewbush said again. 'And another behind that.'

Turning back around, Capstan gazed down at Parade Gardens. It was only half ten in the morning of what was officially "Roman Day", and the place already looked like the entrance to Jengoland during a Bank Holiday Weekend. The entire garden area absolutely heaved with people to the point where he couldn't even see the grass anymore, just a carpet of humanity, all forming one enormous queue that was steadily weaving its way towards the old bandstand on the far right hand side, where a huge sign announced, "ROMAN DAY, REGISTER HERE!"

'Where are all these people coming from?' Capstan asked Dewbush, who'd also turned back to stare down at the assembling masses.

'I've really no idea, Sir.'

'Was it like this last year?'

'Not at all, Sir. Last year you wouldn't have even

known that it was Roman Day!'

There was a pause as they both spent a few moments gazing about.

'Has there been any sign of Becky yet?' asked Capstan.

'I've been looking, Sir, but I haven't spotted her. To be honest, I'm not even sure I've seen a single woman all day. They all appear to be men, Sir.'

Another coach pulled up behind them, and they glanced over to watch as an additional fifty people began to step off it to join more men, from more coaches, all making their way down towards the gardens below.

Capstan looked to his right, and then his left, before whispering to Dewbush, 'Isn't Bath City Police supposed to have forty constables?'

'Yes, Sir. Normally we do.'

'Then why have we only got six?'

'Well, as I mentioned before, Sir, they're all on holiday at the moment, and another four called in sick this morning.'

'Four called in sick?' Capstan repeated. 'Well, I'm not having my men skiving off work just because they've got a bloody hangover. Not today at any rate! Make a note of their names and I'll sack them on Monday.'

'Yes, Sir. Right away, Sir,' and he started to search his pockets for his notebook and pen, whilst trying to work out who wasn't there. Then he saw something unusual.

'Sir, look! A horse box just pulled up. And there are two more behind it!'

'This is totally bloody insane!' Capstan exclaimed.

He'd started to panic. 'There's nothing for it, Dewbush: we need more men!'

'You're probably right, Sir.'

'What do you mean, probably? There's no p*robably* about it! Of course I'm fucking right, you half-brained, dim-witted, spanner-headed twat!'

Capstan took a deep breath in a bid to remain calm. He needed Dewbush now more than ever, and knew he couldn't risk antagonising him too much.

'Sorry, Dewbush. I didn't mean to be rude to you.'

Dewbush was more than a little taken aback. He'd never had a boss apologise to him before, ever, and the fact that this one had only served to highlight the gravity of the situation.

'Dewbush, how about giving Bristol a call? See if they can send some re-enforcements down. It's not supposed to kick off till twelve, so if they can spare some men, they'd still have time to get down here.'

'Yes, Sir. I'll do it now, Sir,' and he fished out his smartphone. 'Um... sorry, Sir. But I don't suppose you have their phone number?'

'Of course I don't have their bloody phone number. Do I look like a telephone directory?'

'No, of course not, Sir. Sorry, Sir.'

'Just Google it, and let me know what they say. Oh, and don't let anyone know what you're doing. I don't want our men becoming overly concerned.'

'Yes, Sir,' said Dewbush, and slunk away to make a discreet but rather desperate call for back-up.

Without anyone to curse, Capstan decided to walk right to the end of the balustrade, further up towards where the registration was taking place, to see if he could spot Becky, but there were just too many people, and without any binoculars they all seemed to merge into one.

By the time he'd walked back again, Dewbush had come off the phone.

'How'd you get on?'

'Very well, Sir. It's all quiet up there, so they said that they can send twenty four men down.'

'Thank God for that! That will give us, what… thirty. Did they say how long it would take for them to arrive?'

'Only a couple of hours, Sir.'

'Well, let's hope nothing happens between now and then. We'll just have to hang around here until they show up.'

Capstan and Dewbush leaned on the balustrade again.

'Look,' Capstan whispered, 'why don't you pop back to the station and dig out a couple of binoculars. That girl's got to be around here somewhere. Maybe if we can find her, we can arrest her, quietly, when nobody's looking. If she is behind all this then it will help to have her locked up and out the way, before the parade kicks off.'

Dewbush thought that that was about the most sensible plan his boss had ever come up with and, relieved to hear that he still seemed calm and in control of the situation, said, 'Yes, Sir. Right away, Sir,' and set off at a brisk pace, back down to the station.

Meanwhile, Capstan paced up and down along the balustrade, keeping an eye on the proceedings whilst looking out for a girl, any girl really, but ideally one who had long dark brown hair, smooth pale skin and a body which most men would happily die for.

Having walked up and down for about ten minutes, he began to realise that after people had registered, down at the bandstand, they were then making their way back up to where he was, beside the balustrade. He also noticed that they were now all carrying identical Safebusy's plastic Bags Forever, which seemed to be crammed full of a variety of peculiar objects, none of which he could make out.

As they began to file past him he was sorely tempted to stop and search a couple of them, just to find out exactly what was in the bags, but there was no way he was going to do anything that might lead to a scene, of any sort. So he kept his hands to himself and stood by, as they started to stream past him, over towards Parade Bridge, which they crossed before disappearing out of sight. Being a police inspector, he was naturally curious to know where they were all going, but decided that with so much going on already, *out of sight* was most definitely *out of mind*, and their absence gave him a lot less to worry about.

CHAPTER XXV
S.P.Q.R.
SENATUS POPULUSQUE ROMANUS
The Senate and People of Rome

AFTER THE PRESS coverage from the previous week, Becky had gone to ground at Mark's house. At that time there was no way for her to know if Capstan had heard about her trip to Bristol. She'd have been surprised if he hadn't, but couldn't be sure. Either way, she didn't want to risk being pulled in for questioning, not with so much still to do, so it made sense for her to temporally move out of her flat, and keep her head down until the big day itself.

She'd also been able to keep a low profile throughout Roman Day's somewhat busy registration period, simply by wearing a khaki green combat jacket and a black baseball cap, both of which she'd borrowed from Mark. She had seen Capstan, high up on Pierrepont Street with Dewbush, both leaning on the balustrade with binoculars, but even though she had a strong feeling that it was her they were looking for, she still felt safe. There were just too many people around for her to be identified. In fact, the only time during that entire morning she'd been even remotely concerned was when she'd had to walk straight past them, on her way over to their base camp. By that time there were considerably more policemen, but her senior officers, the founding members of the Roman Imperialists, were able to keep her from view, as they all strolled along in a group, with Rebecca hidden in the middle.

Once at the camp, after she'd removed her thin disguise, Captain Blankard was able to track her down to re-introduce her to Lord Reginald Anthem, First Lord of the Admiralty, who she still couldn't remember. Lord Anthem, a boisterous old chap, engaged her in a rather animated chat about the now famous party on HMS Britannica before bringing her horse-for-the-day over to meet her. Fury, one of the three Spanish Stallions mentioned in the email, was a truly magnificent animal, and after spending a good ten minutes getting to know him - the horse, not Lord Anthem, who'd been kept busy re-assembling his two gold-plated chariots that had arrived flat-packed - she made her way into her own private marquee, where she prepared herself to lead the procession through the city.

Once inside, she opened her own Safebusy's Bag Forever, one of two thousand they'd ordered along with all the food. Within the bag was her costume, most of which she'd bought online, but it also included the Roman armour she'd be wearing. Having spent several days thinking about it, she'd eventually decided to buy a dark brown steel-boned leather corset, a pair of tan jodhpurs, some brown leather riding boots, and a horse whip. The pièce de résistance was a beautifully ornate silver and gold Roman helmet with an immaculate high red plume in such perfect condition that the whole thing looked like it had just arrived from the British Museum. She could only guess that it had been made for some famous Roman general, and although the fitting was a little loose, she could use her hair to hold it firmly in place.

After she finished dressing, she emerged from the marquee with her riding whip in one hand and the helmet in the other. Mark, Doughnut, Johnno, Sebastian, Captain Blankard, and Lord Anthem were all waiting outside, looking magnificent in their own pristine Roman Army uniforms.

Mark stepped forward to present her with a sword, already sheathed with a dark brown leather belt attached. It was the same sword that Bath's City Police Chief Forensics Officer, Paul Batter, had found when they'd first discovered the haul at the Basin Museum, and after Mark had spent a good half an hour polishing it, the jewel-encrusted hilt now dazzled in the bright light of another cloudless summer's day.

'This is for you, Rebecca.' he said, bowing in reverence.

Smiling with gracious approval, she took it from him and pulled it half out from its sheath, twisting it through the light to admire its beauty. With a smile of satisfaction, she pushed it back and fastened the belt around her waist. Leaning forwards, she eased her head into her helmet before turning back to Mark and the other officers.

'How do I look?'

Mark, like the others, gazed at her in awe.

'Rebecca, you are truly magnificent, like Athena, the

Goddess of War herself!'

They all agreed, and she beamed back at them. Adjusting her sword, so that it rested more comfortably against her thigh, she said, 'Right then. Is everyone ready?'

'I'd say so,' answered Captain Blankard, looking around. 'It's difficult to tell really, but if we sound the horn, as planned, then I suspect those who aren't will soon fall in.'

Rebecca made her way over to where Fury stood, breathing quietly. After giving him a few firm strokes, she took hold of his reins in one hand, held the saddle in the other, lifted her left foot into the stirrup, and heaved herself up to sit high above her cohort of officers.

'OK boys, this is it! Sound the horn and we'll make our way out.'

Doughnut grinned. He'd been waiting for this moment for months, years even, and lifted his very own Cornu up to his mouth and delivered a sound that would have struck fear into the heart of even the bravest Celtic warrior.

They all listened as the hollow note echoed out around them.

The land became still.

Then a rumble swelled up from the ground, and the earth itself trembled, as more than two thousand fully armed Roman Centurions began making their way out for the start of Bath's annual Roman Day Parade.

Leading the way, Rebecca walked Fury past a couple of tennis courts and onto a small tree lined path that led up to North Parade Road. When she reached the junction at the top, she stopped and glanced behind her, to make sure everyone was in their correct positions. She looked left and right, to check that there were no cars coming, and led them out onto the road.

As she ambled up with Fury towards the bridge at the far end, the two chariots fell in behind her, lining up side by side, one with Mark, Doughnut and their charioteer, the other with Captain Blankard and Lord Anthem holding the reins. Following behind came Johnno and Sebastian, both carrying Roman Standards with ornately carved golden eagles perched on top and S.P.Q.R. written underneath; and after them came all the foot soldiers.

Looking up ahead, Rebecca could just about make out Inspector Capstan, who seemed to be walking towards them from the other side of the bridge with Dewbush at his side and a good-sized group of uniformed policemen behind them. From her high vantage point she could also see a television news van parked up with a satellite dish on top and a bustling number of reporters nearby.

Smiling she said to herself, 'Now, this is going to be fun!' and shifted around in her saddle to look behind her again. Her Charioteers and Standard Bearers were all still there, along with a growing number of Centurions, oozing out onto North Parade Road like molten rock spewing from a volcano. Beaming at them all she faced forwards once more as they made their way towards the bridge and the policemen, who'd now formed a human barrier half way across.

Rebecca walked Fury up towards them.

'Oh, look, it's Cat Spam and Bush Dew!'

Leaning back in her saddle, and with a light pull on the reins, she brought Fury to a halt.

'Long time no see! I've missed you both.'

Then, looking at Dewbush, she asked, 'How's the wig?'

Dewbush didn't answer as he'd gone bright red and was staring at the ground.

'That's quite enough of all that, Miss Philips,' said Capstan, keen to take an early command of the situation.

'Oh, don't be so dull, Cat Spam, I was just having a bit of fun.'

Capstan got straight down to business.

'Miss Philips, we're here to arrest you on suspicion of murder, armed robbery, grand theft, handling stolen goods and... what? What is it Dewbush? Can't you see I'm busy?'

Dewbush had been pulling down on Capstan's trench coat in a bid to gain his attention.

'Sir,' he said, with some urgency, 'I thought you said you were going to do this quietly, when nobody was looking!'

'Well, it's too late for that now. Where was I?'

'I think you were about to arrest me,' answered Rebecca, playing with Fury's mane.

'Oh yes, that's right. Rebecca Philips, I hereby arrest you on suspicion of murder, armed robbery, grand theft, handling stolen goods and indecent exposure.'

'What the hell is going on?' cried Lord Anthem from the back. He wasn't used to being held up, by the police or anyone else.

'Oh yes,' Capstan continued, 'and for organising a mass march without the council's permission.'

'Ah, sorry, I thought we'd spoken to them.'

Capstan sneered. 'Apparently not! And now you're just going to have to send that lot back to wherever it was that you dug them up from.'

'Oh well, I suppose if you have to arrest me and stop the parade, then we'd better call it a day,' she said, looking rather despondent. 'Let me just break the bad news to everyone.'

Bringing Fury around, so that she could speak to her army of followers, she sat high in her saddle and began to address them.

'Citizens of Bath, Bristol and beyond,' her voice rang out with noble authority. 'We have gathered here today to celebrate what has become known as Roman Day.'

There was a rippling murmur, as everyone told each other to shut up and keep their swords still.

'Many of you have journeyed far and wide to be with us today, and for that I thank you.'

The gathered masses fell silent, as they stayed as still as possible so that they could hear what their leader had to say.

'Roman Day is not just any day. Roman Day is our day! To remember our ancestors. Those who came here from Rome itself. Those who traversed land and sea, to bring civilisation to our very door. Today is our day to remember those who built the roads, those who built the aqueducts, those who built the drains and the sewage systems. Those who gave us wine to drink and baths to bathe in. Those who brought us a new way of life and, in turn, those who helped make Britain the great nation that it is today.'

A wave of approval rang out as she continued.

'The police, standing here before us, have come to

stop us from marching.'

A more malevolent murmur followed.

'They have even ordered you back to your homes.'

The murmur became a quiet rumble.

Rebecca paused to let her army become silent again.

'They have also come to arrest me.'

The silence grew cold.

'And to take me away from you.'

Her words hung in the air, and the army became deathly still.

In the oppressive silence she walked Fury around, so that she could talk to Capstan again. Having made the full circle she leaned down and asked him with a clear, soft voice. 'Are you really sure you want to be doing this?'

Capstan was having second thoughts. Even the horses had fallen silent and all he could hear was the water running under the bridge and his heart beating behind his ears. He gulped as a sense of dread spread out through his body. But now was not the time for fear. He was a policeman, through and through, and having spent the last few weeks being insulted, humiliated and pushed around by this girl, he now had her exactly where he wanted her, and with thirty police constables in place to back him up, there was absolutely no way he was going to let her get away from him this time.

Taking a deep breath he said, 'Now look, Miss Philips...' but she'd already turned the horse round and had started to address her followers again.

'But I say to you that it is our right - no, it is our duty to march, in honour of our ancestors, for those who sacrificed so much to give us the life that we now lead, and that we can now pass on to our children.'

'Miss Philips, I suggest you climb down off that horse and come quietly, before there's any trouble.'

Rebecca pulled Fury around again to glower at him with a look of demonic intensity.

'I'm not finished yet!' she said, and turned back to stare out over the mass of people lining the road behind them.

She gazed deep into some of their many faces as they all looked back at her, transfixed by her majestic beauty and the raw sexual power that oozed from her every pore.

They awaited her command.

'Christ!' said Capstan, quietly to himself.

Dewbush butted in.

'Sir, I really think we should be doing this later, when we have more men. A lot more men! Really, I do, Sir!'

'Not now, Dewbush.'

Capstan had made up his mind, for better or worse, and was not going to be persuaded otherwise.

Feeling increasingly unwell, Dewbush made the executive decision to start edging backwards, away from what looked to him like an insurmountable force and one that was most definitely not to be trifled with.

Girding his loins, as best he could anyway, and keeping his eyes fixed on Rebecca ahead, Capstan spoke back to those behind him.

'Hold your ground, men! She's not getting away from us this time.'

Had he thought to look back, he would have observed that his police unit were struggling to hold onto the contents of their bowels, let alone the ground they stood on, and were all following their Sergeant's example, by trying to put as much distance between themselves and the heavily armed Roman force that stood before them, without anyone noticing.

Rebecca again sat high in her saddle. Taking a firm grasp of her jewel studded sword she cried out, 'I AM REBECCA OF BATH, HEAR MY VOICE!'

In the stillness that followed, she unsheathed the sword, held it high in the air and screamed, 'CHAAAARRRRGGGGGE!'

A great roar lifted off the ground and thundered overhead, as over two thousand men pulled out their own swords and joined in the battle cry.

Rebecca heaved Fury back to rear up, full height; and the other stallions joined in.

Capstan found himself unable to move, as the blood drained from his face and the contents of his bladder did something similar. It was Dewbush who called the retreat.

'RUN FOR YOUR LIVES, MEN! RUN FOR YOUR LIVES!'

His fellow policemen didn't need to be told twice, and started falling backwards over themselves in a desperate bid to escape from what they considered to be certain death.

Seeing his boss just standing there, Dewbush grabbed his trench coat and heaved him back, but it was too late for all of them, as Rebecca's horse slammed into the fleeing group, knocking them sideways like thirty two pins in a bowling alley, straight into the path of the on-coming chariots that ran straight over them.

And as they all lay there, splattered out over the

road, the foot soldiers spent the next ten minutes treading on them as they forged their way over the bridge.

The army continued their charge and drove into the TV camera crew, who'd all been so immersed with their filming that they'd forgotten the first two rules of journalism: not to allow themselves to become emotionally involved and never, under any circumstances, to stand in the path of an invading Roman army.

With shoppers scattering and tourists fleeing, the armed mass surged towards York Street where they tore past the Roman Basin Museum and started to make their way up to where Johnno's Mum lived for a nice cup of tea and a cream bun.

CHAPTER XXVI
HONESTAM VENATUS
A decent game

ROBERT BRIDLESTOCK sat down at his desk at Number 10, coffee in one hand and the latest edition of Golf Club Owners Magazine in the other. He was in a buoyant mood and was looking forward to sitting down for a few minutes before his Private Secretary came in to bombard him with his rather dull itinerary for the day, as he had a nasty habit of doing. He did enjoy being Prime Minister. After all, he was the most important man in the United Kingdom, and one of the most influential on Planet Earth; but the job itself was all rather tedious, and if someone had told him that it only came with a salary of £142,000 a year, he doubted he'd have bothered getting himself elected in the first place. Considering the amount of responsibility he had, he honestly thought that he was the most underpaid person in the country - well, in London at any rate.

But he'd made the best of a bad thing and, having just come to the end of his first term in office, thought it had all gone rather well, all things considered. The oil companies had been far more generous than he was expecting in the run up to passing the Pro-Fracking Bill, and the North Korean Government had paid a decent sum into his offshore account as a finder's fee for their new Chief Nuclear Science Officer, who Robert had personally recommended; but these paled in comparison to the hefty deposits made by all the major international banking corporations to keep the Chancellor of the Exchequer away from their own offshore reserves. With a few other global corporations throwing him the odd bone for similar services, since starting the job he'd been able to increase his net worth to over £540 million, tax free!

So, with that in mind, he'd decided to buy himself a golf club and had asked his valet to pick up the magazine that he was now keen to spend a few minutes reading.

Opening the front page he smiled to himself, thinking of all those sad, middle-class golfers out there who'd bought the magazine thinking that it was the perfect place to find a new set of clubs, when it was of course golf's version of Country Life, and was for people of breeding, and money, like himself, who were looking for a new golf club, singular. He had a garage stacked full of clubs; what he needed was a decent sized course to play on, without having to put up with those less privileged than himself who couldn't afford to buy their own.

On the fifth page he found what he thought might be suitable; a thirty-five acre country golf estate in Hertfordshire, with eighteen holes and a swimming pool, and for only £42 million. He was about to pick up the phone to call the estate agent when his Private Secretary, Fredrick Overtoun, walked in looking almost rushed, with a stack of newspapers under both arms.

'Good morning, Prime Minister, I hope you had a good weekend?'

'Oh, hello, Freddy. Yes, thank you! I managed ten

over par on Saturday and nine over on Sunday, and more to the point, I beat that bloody Henry Flavourington both times!'

'Well done, Prime Minister!'

'Thank you. And you?'

He obviously wasn't interested in how his Private Secretary's weekend was, but thought he should ask, out of politeness.

'Yes, quite pleasant, Prime Minister, thank you; but on a more important note, I don't suppose you heard about Bath over the weekend?'

'No, what about it? It's not leaking again is it? For God's sake! I'm the Prime Minister of the most important country in the world. You'd think that someone would be able to find me a plumber who could stop the damn thing from dripping into the kitchen.'

'Er, no, Prime Minister. I meant Bath, the city.'

'Oh, no, I hadn't.' He stared up at the corner of his office ceiling and said, 'Utinam spatiere loco potes dicere umquam,' before looking back down at his magazine again.

'I'm sorry, Prime Minister, my Latin is still a little rusty.'

Robert looked back up at his Private Secretary.

'Yes, of course. Sorry! I keep forgetting that you didn't go to Cambridge. I was just saying that I haven't heard of the place. I can only assume that they don't have any decent golf courses there. Is it up north somewhere?'

Fredrick had never been able to fully understand just exactly how Robert Bridlestock had managed to become Prime Minister. Yes, he was a good looking man, for his age, and he could certainly deliver a good speech, but he knew absolutely nothing about anything really, except golf, and he was hardly the sharpest tool in the box. The only thing he did seem to have going for him was that he'd read Latin at Cambridge, not Law, as was the norm for politicians, and was subsequently able to recite the ancient language at the drop of a hat, or more importantly, in response to an awkward question. So, all those who'd only got as far as a long weekend in Florence, like himself, were left suitably impressed and with the assumption that anyone who could converse so naturally in such a highbrow, scholastic language, must therefore have a natural aptitude for leading a country.

'Er, no, Prime Minister. It's a city over near Bristol, on the west coast of the mainland,' and then added, 'near Wales,' in an effort to help the PM work out where it was.

But Robert had already returned to reading his magazine. He couldn't see how any of this had anything to do with him. He'd at least heard of Bristol, but knew for a fact that there weren't any decent golf courses there.

A few moments later he looked up to see that his Private Secretary was still standing next to him, which was all rather annoying, especially as he'd just found another country golf estate in Kent that looked even more promising.

'Look, Freddy, I am rather busy at the moment, as you can see,' and he showed him the magazine. 'Are you going to tell me about what happened in Bath or are you just going to stand there all day looking like you're waiting to start a paper round?'

'Yes, Prime Minister, I mean no, Prime Minister. Prime Minister, it would appear that the City of Bath has fallen back under Roman occupation.'

'I'm sorry, I'm not with you.'

'Bath, Prime Minister. It's fallen back under Roman occupation.'

'How can Bath fall back under Roman occupation? Didn't all the Romans bugger off back to Italy in the Dark Ages?'

By "Dark Ages" he meant, of course, before the game of golf had been invented.

'Yes, well, according to the press, they're back, having reinvaded on Saturday afternoon.'

'I've never heard so much rubbish in all my life! What the hell are you talking about? Are you drunk?'

Fredrick was, a little, but didn't think that it was relevant.

'No, Prime Minister. It's all over the news. The press are having a field day!'

It was then that Fredrick handed him Sunday's issue of The Sun, the newspaper that Number 10 always referred to when looking to find out what mattered most to their electorate.

There, sprawled out over the front page, was a picture of Rebecca, in full armour, rearing up on Fury with policeman scattering in front of her, and underneath, in block capitals: BATH BATTERED BY ROMAN MARAUDERS

'This is just another typically stupid, over-the-top Sun headline, surely?'

'Apparently not, Prime Minister. Here's the story again in The Sunday Telegraph, The Mail on Sunday, The Sunday Observer, The Sunday Times and The

Sunday Express,' Fredrick said, as he began pulling out all the papers from under his left arm to pile them up on the Prime Minister's desk.

'What about the F.T.?'

As far as Robert was concerned, if it wasn't in The Financial Times, it wasn't worth mentioning.'

But Fredrick was aware of this, and pulled that one out last.

'Yes, Prime Minister, front page again! And there's some rather alarming footage on the BBC's website, of the very moment the invasion took place.'

Prepared as always, Fredrick pulled out his iPhone and began to play the film from the television camera that had not only captured the moment Capstan and his men had been run over by Fury and the two chariots, but had also continued filming after it had been knocked to the ground a few moments later, and the subsequent ten minutes of endless numbers of feet going past, made for compelling viewing.

Robert watched the stampede with his mouth half open and, for once, speechless, so Fredrick thought he'd continue, whilst he had the chance.

'It's gone out on YouTube as well, Prime Minister, and has already been viewed over a million times.'

A response was still not forthcoming, so Fredrick carried on.

'And it gets worse, I'm afraid, Prime Minister,' and he started to take out all the newspapers from under his other arm and began piling them up on the desk as well.

'As you can see, all of today's papers feature a picture of you, playing golf, whilst the City of Bath has been forced to declare that it has, indeed, fallen back under Roman occupation.'

Robert was finally drawn out of his silent contemplation as he stared down at one particular series of pictures that showed a moment-by-moment breakdown of his swing.

'You know what,' he eventually said, 'I think those were taken of me on the seventeenth tee. I'd just had a tremendous drive, right down the middle, and was looking at two shots for a birdie.'

'Yes, Prime Minister, but the papers are all saying that whilst our country is being re-invaded by Romans, you're out playing golf!'

'So bloody what! I always play golf on Sundays. Doesn't everyone?'

'Possibly not, Prime Minister. Furthermore, an armed force of an estimated one thousand Roman soldiers was observed marching up the A4 towards Bristol, late on Sunday morning.'

Now that did get the Prime Minister's attention.

'This really is quite serious, isn't it, Freddy?'

'I'm afraid so, Prime Minister.'

'Right, get General Hillander-Moss on the phone. He'll know what to do.'

'But what about the Cabinet, Prime Minister? Shouldn't you speak to them about it first?'

'Sod the Cabinet! I've never met such a bunch of Girl Guides in all my life, and anyway, they're all bloody lawyers. I need to speak to someone who can give me some useful military advice.'

Having learnt a long time before never to argue with the Prime Minister, Fredrick had already picked up the phone and, after just a few moments, said, 'He's on the line for you now, Prime Minister.'

'Good work, Freddy. Now we'll see what's really going on,' and he snatched the phone out of Fredrick's hand before leaning back in his black leather executive's chair.

'Mossy my boy! How are you, my good man? Yes, fine thank you. Really? Not bad, not bad at all! I got nine over on Sunday. Well, we'll have to play again sometime. That's right! Now listen, what's all this I hear about a so-called Roman invasion?'

The office fell silent as the PM listened, and only interrupted the General with the occasional, 'I see.'

After about five minutes he said, 'Clama cladem belli occasionem canibus!' before roaring with laughter and putting the phone down. He then picked up that morning's Observer, which happened to be on top of the pile, and said, 'I must say, I do look rather good. My swing has definitely improved.'

'Prime Minister, may I ask what General Hillander-Moss had to say?'

'Oh, yes of course, sorry. He's going to send a field battalion over to Bath to have a look around.'

'He's going to do what?'

Fredrick was looking even less composed than he'd done when he first walked in.

'A field battalion, over to Bath. He thinks that if they can see we mean business, they'll call it a day.'

'But, Prime Minister, you can't just send an armed force over there without asking the Cabinet first!'

As the ramifications of what could happen began to sink in, Fredrick was turning increasingly pale.

'Don't worry, Freddy, for Christ's sake! They're not going to launch an all-out attack or anything, and if anyone asks what they're up to, they're just going to say that they're on a training exercise. Look, they should be in their positions by midday, at which point Mossy promised to give me a call and tell me exactly what's what, so, whilst all that's going on, I'm going to take an early lunch.'

And with that, he pushed himself away from his desk, stood up and started peering under the piles of newspapers for his golf magazine.

'Just leave whatever else it is that you want me to do today on my desk and I'll look at it when I get back, there's a good chap.'

Then he gave Fredrick a brief smile, patted his shoulder, and headed upstairs to his private apartment. Having now seen so many pictures of his golf swing, he was certain it had improved, and was more determined than ever to buy himself a decent sized course; and the one down in Kent looked like it had his name written all over it.

CHAPTER XXVII
IDUS AUGUSTI
The Ides of August

JUST AS THE Prime Minister was standing up to find somewhere quieter to read his magazine, Rebecca was sitting down, still in her Roman uniform, to write Capstan and his men a Get Well Soon card. She'd meant to do it sooner, but had been so busy with everything that it had slipped her mind.

'Mark, what do you think I should write?'

'I've no idea. Are you sure they're still alive?' he said, with a smirk.

'Yes, I think so. Well, they were when I phoned the hospital yesterday. They said that they just have cuts and bruises, mainly. A few have hairline fractures, and some have broken bones; arms, legs, ribs, that sort of thing. Concussion was also mentioned, along with internal haemorrhaging, but I've been assured that they'll all be up and about at some point, most of them at least. How about I write, "Sorry I stampeded over you, and all your men, on Saturday; and everyone else is very sorry too."?'

'Maybe it would be better if it was less... factual?'

She put her pen to her mouth, thought about it for a moment and then scrawled out, 'Dear Cat Spam, I hope you're feeling better, and say hello to Bush Dew for me. Love and hugs, Rebecca of Bath."

'That will do,' she said to herself, and then addressed the envelope to "Inspector Capstan, c/o

The Royal United Hospital, Bath," before stuffing the card inside and strolling over to her marquee's entrance to pass it to the Centurion standing guard outside.

'Could you hand-deliver that for me? And maybe pick up some flowers and chocolate for him on the way?'

'Yes, Ma'am.'

Feeling slightly less guilty, she returned to help Mark unpack.

The previous morning, Bath's Rugby Club had asked if it would be possible for them to move, as they had a match that afternoon; but as they were all having such a good time, instead of going home they'd simply relocated their base camp to Parade Gardens on the other side of the river.

With regret, they had to say goodbye to Captain Blankard and a thousand of his men, as they needed to get back to their ship for Monday morning, but Blankard had allowed the remainder to stay on for a period of extended leave. Out of gratitude for all their support, she'd let them keep their Roman Centurion uniforms. They were all from YouGet, apart from Blankard's, so it was no great loss, but the gesture had been well received, especially when she said that they could take their L Plates off. And in the spirit of the occasion, they'd all decided to march the thirty four miles back to their ship, instead of using the fleet of coaches they'd arrived in.

With nothing better to do, Lord Reginald Anthem had decided he'd stay on for a while as well, along with his horses and staff, for a few more days at least. Rebecca didn't mind at all. The old man had turned out to be both highly intelligent and great fun to be with, and he knew a surprising amount about Roman history, so she'd given him the marquee next to hers.

At around eleven o'clock, Lord Anthem appeared outside her tent.

'Rebecca, my dear, do you have a moment?'

'Yes, of course Reggie, come in! I've had enough of unpacking anyway.'

'I'm afraid there's news from the other side of the river.'

'Oh really? What's that?'

Mark looked up as well.

'An Army battalion is positioning itself opposite, in the recreational grounds. There do seem to be quite a few of them, and they seem to have brought some field artillery with them as well.'

Rebecca smiled to herself. It did sound serious, but she couldn't help but find it amusing.

'Let's have a look!' she said, and strode out, with Mark following behind.

The three of them headed over to the bandstand, where they'd have a more elevated view.

'You can just make them out,' Lord Anthem said, peering through his binoculars.

'May I?' Rebecca asked.

'Yes, of course.'

Through the trees she could just about see a number of field guns being positioned all along the far bank, with khaki green tents already erected in the playing fields behind.

After a few moments, she passed them to Mark.

'Take a look. What do you think?'

He scanned the scene. 'Well, they've got some big

guns alright. I can see about six.'

'Any idea what we're looking at, Reggie?'

'It's a Royal Artillery battalion, probably around three hundred personnel. Those are their L118 Howitzers. They have one hundred and five millimetre barrels, an automatic pointing system, need a crew of six, can fire up to eight rounds per minute, and have a range of just over eighteen thousand yards.'

'You're kidding?' Rebecca said, impressed, but with some concern.

'Unfortunately not, Rebecca. I've never liked those Army bods and it does look like they mean business.'

'But I don't understand. Why are they here?'

'Did you not see the papers?' Lord Anthem asked.

'No, she doesn't "do" the news,' said Mark, rolling his eyes.

'Well, they're all saying that Bath's fallen back under Roman occupation.' Rebecca snorted with laughter. 'Utter hogwash I know, but that's the British press for you!'

Mark began to look increasingly uneasy, and started shifting from one foot to the other.

'Perhaps we should just pack up and go home?' he suggested.

'Why?' demanded Rebecca. 'Apart from running over a few stupid policemen, we've done nothing wrong!'

'We did put some journalists in hospital as well,' Mark pointed out.

'I'm not sure they count, and anyway, the local council said that it was the best Roman Day they'd ever had, and gave us their permission to camp here for a few days. As far as they're concerned, they think we're just what the local tourist industry needs.'

'I'm sure your right my dear,' agreed Lord Anthem, 'but it may be worthwhile calling it a day. After all, it's not worth anyone getting killed over.'

Rebecca thought about it for a few moments. She'd gained a huge respect for Lord Anthem over the past couple of days. He clearly knew what he was talking about and it was probably sensible to heed his advice.

'I suppose you're right. Look, let's have one final banquet and then we'll pack up afterwards. Mark, what's Doughnut up to?'

'He's started teaching Roman Army battle manoeuvres to a group from the Britannica.'

'How about the others?'

'I don't know.'

'Well, find whoever you can and go and pick us up some more food, will you? Another thousand quarter pounders should cover it, and a few kegs of Bath's Best. Oh, and just go straight to the cash and carry this time. Safebusy's seem to struggle with orders by the tonne.'

'No problem,' and Mark headed off to find his friends. He didn't feel comfortable being in quite such close proximity to Her Majesty's Armed Forces, and although shopping was hardly his favourite pastime, it was at least preferable to being in the direct line of fire of six field guns and three hundred armed military personnel.

'Reggie, do you think we could walk the horses around the camp for a while? I'm missing Fury. Such a magnificent animal.'

'I was about to suggest the very same thing, my dear. They really should be ridden every day. We'll take all three out. I'll have one of our charioteers join us, but may I suggest that we first post a couple of scouts on the river bank, to keep an eye on what's going on over the other side, just to be safe?'

And so it was, that Rebecca of Bath and Lord Reginald Anthem, First Lord of the Admiralty, were joined by Cedric, Lord Anthem's Chief Charioteer, as they rode their three majestic white Spanish Stallions through the hustle and bustle of their Roman Army camp. Occasionally they'd stop to watch life unfold. One group was having an arm wrestling competition, another a boisterous game of cards, but most were just chatting as they polished their swords and shields outside their tents.

It wasn't long before they ambled up to Doughnut, who was busy managing three groups as they practised spear throwing, sword fighting and the ever-challenging Tortoise Shell shield manoeuvre.

'How are they doing?' Rebecca asked him.

'Bloody well! They've only been training for an hour and they're already better than us.'

Everywhere they looked, people were happy. Even the television camera crew that had been wandering around the camp interviewing people seemed cheerful, and the balustrade above bustled with tourists, all taking pictures and video of what must have looked like a re-make of *Ben-Hur*.

And when Mark returned with Sebastian, Johnno and the others from their bus trip to the cash and carry, fires were lit, burgers were cooked, jokes were told and songs were sung; and as smoke drifted high above the camp the three riders took a burger each and headed up to the balustrade on Pierrepont Street to enjoy a more panoramic view, and to also keep an eye on what looked to be some more movement among the Royal Artillery battalion beyond.

CHAPTER XXVIII
QUID AGIS HODIE?
How are you?

'HE'S ON THE line for you now, Prime Minister.'

Having had Fredrick, his Private Secretary, call up to his flat to let him know when General Hillander-Moss was in position, Robert Bridlestock had trundled his way back down to his office. He'd spent a good few hours reading his golf magazine whilst watching the cricket on TV, and having arranged a viewing of the country golf estate in Kent, he felt he'd actually achieved something worthwhile for a change.

As he closed his office door behind him he said, 'Thank you, Freddy. Oh, hello Gerry? What are you doing here?'

Fredrick had taken a political risk by informing Gerald Frackenburger, the Defence Minister, of the situation, and had asked him to attend, so he thought he'd better explain why he'd done so without his boss's permission.

'Prime Minister, I thought it may be wise for you to have your Defence Minister present during the conversation with General Hillander-Moss.'

'Well, yes, fair enough.'

'And that maybe we could use the speaker phone this time, so that he's able to join in the conversation.'

'Yes, yes, very well, very well, if we must!'

Gerald Frackenburger, who was standing rather

awkwardly in the middle of the room, said, 'I hear, Prime Minister, that you've mobilised our Armed Forces in response to the Roman Army threat in Bath.'

'Look Gerry, I understand your concern, really I do, but all I've done is ask Hillander-Moss to pop over to have a look.'

'I'm sorry Prime Minister, but it's Parliamentary law to seek permission from the House before actively engaging our Armed Forces, especially when it concerns a sensitive domestic issue, such as this.'

The Defence Minister wasn't too bothered about the House not being asked; he was a little more miffed that he, personally, had been excluded from the decision.

'Look, honestly Gerry, there really is no need for concern. Quite frankly, I don't even know why you're here.' He then gave his Private Secretary a very hard stare, and Fredrick looked down at the ornate Persian rug under his feet. 'But anyway, now that you are, you may as well stick around. Put the General on, will you please, Freddy?'

'Yes, Prime Minister,' and Fredrick, phone in hand, leaned forward to switch the speaker on before saying, 'The Prime Minister is here for you now, General.'

'Good afternoon Prime Minister, Quid agis hodie?'

'Valde bene gratias tibi aget. Quomodo suus tempestas?'

Robert really enjoyed his conversations with Hillander-Moss as he was one of the few people he still kept in touch with who'd also read Latin at Cambridge.

'Rather good actually!' answered the General. 'There are a few clouds dotted about and we do have a slight cross-wind, but apart from that, it's another perfect British summer's day.'

'Good stuff. And who did you decide to bring with you in the end?'

'Oh, just some chaps from the Royal Artillery. They were training in the Brecon Beacons, so it didn't take them long to make their way down.'

'Well, that all sounds fine,' Robert said and smiled round at Frackenburger. 'Listen, Mossy, we have Gerry here, the Defence Minister, who'd like to join in with our conversation.'

'Oh, hello, Gerry. Quid agis hodie?'

Gerald looked over at Robert for help.

'Mossy, I don't think Gerry went to Cambridge.'

'Ah, sorry Gerry. I was just asking how you were.'

Gerald disliked with a high degree of intensity being called "Gerry" all the time by pompous arrogant pricks who considered themselves to be better than everyone else simply because their parents could afford to send them to Cambridge, and because they could converse in a language that had been dead for over five hundred years.

'Oh, fine, thank you, General,' he answered, doing well to hide his contempt. 'May I ask if you can see the Roman insurgents?'

'Yes, we can see them alright, although the view is slightly obscured.'

'How many of them would you say there are?' the Defence Minister asked.

'It's difficult to tell really, but I'd say roughly about a thousand, give or take a few hundred.'

'And how many men do you have?'

'Just the one battalion.'

Robert joined in. 'And how many are in a battalion Mossy, about ten?'

'No, Prime Minister. We have three hundred armed personnel in total along with six Howitzers, all lined up and ready to fire.'

'Oh!' said Robert, with a surprised look on his face. He then glanced over at his Defence Minister and asked, quietly, 'What's a Howitzer?'

Gerald glared at him. 'It's a very large field gun, Prime Minister!'

'Ah, I see!'

Robert was just beginning to wonder if involving his old university chum in this was such a good idea after all. He leaned in towards the speaker phone again and asked, 'What's the Roman Army doing now, Mossy?'

'They're all just sitting around, Prime Minister. It looks like they're having a barbecue.'

'Do you think they pose any sort of imminent threat?'

'Well, they don't have any modern weaponry, just swords and shields mainly, so I'd say probably not.'

Robert stood up and smiled back at both the Defence Minister and his Private Secretary again.

'You see, I told you! There's absolutely nothing to worry about.'

Clearly neither was convinced, so Robert turned back to the speaker phone and, half-joking, said, 'Well, don't fire then, for Christ's sake!' and tilted his head back to wink at the Defence Minister.

'Are you sure, Prime Minister?' asked the General.

'Yes, of course I'm bloody sure!'

'Right you are.'

There was a brief pause and then, in the background, they heard someone shout, 'OPEN FIRE!'

In shock, the three of them just stood there, mouths agog, as a huge discharge of heavy artillery began to erupt from the speaker phone that sat harmlessly on the Prime Minister's desk.

Moments later, the General's voice came blaring out. 'THEY'RE FIRING NOW, PRIME MINISTER.'

Just to be heard over the ensuing noise, Robert was forced to shout.

'YES, WE CAN HEAR THAT. NOW STOP FIRING! FOR GOD'S SAKE, STOP FIRING!'

'BUT YOU JUST TOLD ME TO OPEN FIRE!'

'I SAID DON'T FIRE, YOU BLOODY IDIOT, DON'T FIRE!!!'

'OH, SORRY. HOLD ON. BEAR WITH ME. IT ALWAYS TAKES THEM A WHILE TO STOP ONCE THEY'VE STARTED.'

'JUST TELL THEM TO STOP FIRING! PLEASE GOD, STOP FIRING!!!'

In the background they could hear the General calling out, 'CEASE FIRE MEN! CEASE FIRE!' and as word spread, the guns began to fall silent, as did the phone.

'Are you still there, General? General?'

'Yes, sorry, Prime Minister. I was just looking to see if we were able to hit anything.'

The speaker phone then cracked loudly and went dead.

'General? GENERAL? CAN YOU HEAR ME, GENERAL?'

CHAPTER XXIX
CASULATIES BELLI
Casualties of War

'GOD HELP US!' exclaimed Lord Anthem.

Rebecca gave him a bewildered look as he sat bolt upright on the horse next to hers. Then she watched him throw his half-eaten hamburger to the pavement, just missing a tourist, to put both hands around his mouth and shout, 'GET DOWN EVERYONE! GET DOWN!!!'

Confused, she looked back at the camp where she saw the two Centurions who'd been posted as lookouts, make a break from the tree line beside the river.

The bandstand exploded.

Fury went berserk, as did the two other Spanish Stallions, and reared up to full height, but as Rebecca had been using both hands to eat she was unable to hold on and was thrown backwards, onto the pavement, putting a dent in her precious Roman helmet. And as she fell, another explosion erupted from the gardens below, closely followed by four more.

Her horse galloped off at full speed through crowds of panicking tourists, who were all now taking cover, and pictures, from behind the solid stone balustrade. The other two stallions followed suit, leaving only Cedric clinging on to his mount for dear life. Lord Anthem had suffered a similar fate to Rebecca and now lay, badly hurt, beside her.

'What the hell is going on?' she asked him.

'It's the Howitzers. They've opened fire!'

Keeping her head as low as possible, she crawled over to peer through the balustrade to see for herself, and just as she did, another three explosions erupted, one after the other, and each one shaking the ground beneath her. She was now desperate to find Mark and the others, but the camp was being torn to shreds and all she could see was smoke, earth and hundreds of indistinguishable Centurions, all taking cover behind their shields.

'A phone?'

Rebecca glanced behind her to see Lord Anthem, in some pain, stretching his hand out towards her.

'A phone? Do you have a phone?' he managed, before slumping back to the pavement as the gardens took another pounding.

She didn't. She'd left all that sort of thing in her tent, but could see the urgency of his plea and looked over at a Japanese tourist lying flat on his stomach beside her, taking a series of frenzied photographs through the balustrade's pillars. She gave him a hard prod and shouted, 'CAN I BORROW YOUR PHONE? A PHONE?' sticking out her thumb and little finger to imitate one.

He smiled at her, pulled out his iPhone and handed it over, shouting, 'HAI, DOZO.' as more shells exploded.

She returned the smile and gave the phone to Lord Anthem who pushed himself up from the ground, and dialled frantically before holding it to his ear.

'Captain Blankard, this is Lord Reginald Anthem.

Listen, no time to talk. We're under heavy bombardment by the British Army!'

Another series of explosions erupted beneath them.

'I've really no idea why, but I need you to launch your two Sea Darts at the Recreational Grounds, where we were camping yesterday. No, you'll have to look up the coordinates. I repeat, LAUNCH BOTH SEA DARTS AT THE RECREATIONAL GROUNDS. Yes, as First Lord of the Admiralty you have the British Navy's full authorisation, but hurry man, we're being cut to pieces!'

Exhausted, he slumped back down.

Rebecca wasn't too sure what he'd just asked Blankard to do, but whatever it was, she hoped he'd do it soon.

After what seemed like an eternity, the heavy shell fire began to abate, and when she thought it had finally stopped, she started to push herself up to have another look for Mark, but Lord Anthem pulled her back to the ground.

'I'd keep your head down if I were you, my dear.'

Just then they heard a noise that sounded like an approach from the Red Arrows. A bright white light flashed overhead followed by the single biggest explosion Rebecca had ever heard in her entire life. Momentarily the pavement lifted up beneath them and then, as the blast thundered off into the distance, great clods of grass, earth and a number of smoking army boots began to rain down on them from what must have been a great height.

Rebecca looked over again at Lord Anthem, who couldn't help but smile at her.

'You can take a look now,' he said, and started to

push himself upright.

She reached over to help him and, together, they heaved themselves up.

Rebecca stared out. She now had an unobstructed line of sight across the river as there were no more trees left to obscure the view. What had been a series of lush green playing fields that made up Bath's Recreational Grounds, where they'd been camping just the day before, had been replaced by a single, giant smouldering crater.

'What the...?' Rebecca asked, in awe. 'But... where did the Royal Artillery go?'

Lord Anthem looked over at her.

'HMS Britannica is armed with Sea Darts,' he explained. 'Five hundred and fifty kilogram missiles with eleven kilogram warheads. They have a range of over forty miles and travel at twice the speed of sound. Unfortunately for the British Army they make Howitzers look like something you'd find inside a Christmas cracker!'

CHAPTER XXX
POTESNE ME AUDIRE?
Can you hear me?

'GENERAL? GENERAL? GENERAL?'

The Prime Minister was still shouting at the phone but to no avail.

'Fuck it!' he said, and turned to his Private Secretary. 'Fredrick, I need to get up there NOW! Get me a police escort to City Airport and have a helicopter waiting.'

'Yes, Prime Minister,' he said, enjoying the moment.

'Well, don't just stand there saying, "Yes, Prime Minister" all the bloody time. Bring a car around! And until I know exactly what's just happened, I want that place locked down. Do you hear me? LOCKED DOWN! I don't care how you do it, but if an uncensored news report leaks out before I'm on the scene, I'll have your head stuck on a spike outside the Tower of London!'

Fredrick made a swift exit without saying another word, leaving the Defence Minister standing in the middle of the room also looking rather smug.

'And I'll have your head next to his if you don't wipe that smile off your face!'

'Yes, Prime Minister, but you should have listened…'

'I don't give a flying fuck what you think I should have done. As far as I'm concerned, whatever's just happened up there is YOUR FAULT! You're the Defence Minister, so it's your head that will roll, not mine!'

As the Prime Minister's words sank in, Gerald began to imagine his head being used by the world's press for an impromptu football match before being skewered onto a wrought iron spike to enjoy a pleasant view over the Thames.

'Right,' Robert continued, 'grab your coat. You're coming with us!'

'Where to?' asked Gerald, who'd just started to imagine his eyes being plucked out by ravens.

'To Jengoland! Where do you think you moron?'

And with that they left the office, just as the speaker phone began to repeat, 'We're trying to reconnect your call, please hold.'

CHAPTER XXXI
NON QUOD IUSTUM EST?
Isn't that right?

ALREADY THE DISTANT sound of ambulances could be heard as Rebecca stumbled her way over sprawled-out tourists to peer over the balustrade, desperate for some sign of Mark. But what had been, just minutes before, an ornately decorated city park, blossoming with summer flowers and burgeoning with marquees and Roman Centurions, now looked more like the venue for the International Grave Digger of the Year Award, and she couldn't see him anywhere.

It was fairly obvious where the Howitzer shells had fallen, as each was marked by a good-sized crater, but as she made her way down to the gardens, her fear that half her army were all lying dead and just awaited a decent burial were soon allayed. All around her she could see an ever-increasing number of Centurions begin to emerge from behind their shields, shell-shocked and dirty, but otherwise unharmed.

Reaching the first group she asked, 'Are you OK?' and began to help them pull each other out from the layers of earth that they'd been covered in.

'We're all fine, Ma'am, thank you!'

'I can't believe you've all survived!'

'Neither can we, Ma'am,' came their British Bulldog response. And then, through grateful white teeth, they said, 'God bless you, Ma'am!'

She smiled back before asking, 'Has anyone seen Mark, or Doughnut?'

But they hadn't, and so she continued to pick her way through similar scenes, stopping occasionally to pull someone out from a pile of earth and other times to simply offer words of comfort and praise for their resilience in the line of fire. And all the while the same story came back, that everyone seemed to have escaped from what she thought must have been certain death.

'REBECCA! OVER HERE, REBECCA!'

She heard Mark calling and looked around to see him staggering towards her. Running over she gave him a rugby tackle sort of a hug.

'Are you OK?' she asked. 'I was so worried!'

'Yes, I'm fine.'

'And Doughnut, and the others?'

'Yes, they're all fine.'

'Thank God!' and she hugged him again.

'From what I can make out, it looks like we've all made it through in one piece.'

'But I don't understand. From up there it looked like we'd be lucky if we could identify the bodies!'

'It's this Roman armour. Bloody amazing! It can really take a pounding. Even that stuff from YouGet seems to have done the job. As soon as everything kicked off we all just took shelter behind our shields. I think the only way someone could have been seriously hurt was if they'd taken a direct hit.'

'Well, look, get everyone up to the ambulances and have them checked over. I'm going to keep searching for survivors.'

'Do you know what happened yet?' asked Mark. 'We've still got no idea!'

'It was the Royal Artillery. They just opened fire on us for no good reason, and when I find out who gave the order there's going to be hell to pay.'

Bending down to pick up a still smoking beret that he'd seen resting near his foot, Mark asked, 'But where did they all go - the Royal Artillery?' and then he peered inside it, looking for its owner.

'Apparently that was our counter-attack, courtesy of HMS Britannica. Lord Anthem called Blankard and told him to launch a couple of their missiles.'

Still looking confused, Rebecca kissed him and wondered off to continue her circumnavigation of the site, looking out for anyone who'd come off worse than others and helping them up to the fleet of ambulances that now lined Pierrepont Street above.

It was about an hour and a half later, just as she was helping the last of her men into an ambulance, that she saw someone who, despite her very best efforts never to read a newspaper or watch the news, even she could recognise. It was the Prime Minister, crouching down and having what looked like a very frank discussion with Lord Anthem, who was sitting on the back of a St. John's Ambulance with a red blanket over his shoulders.

She strode straight over.

'Are you responsible for this?' she asked, gesticulating down at what looked like a World War One field hospital.

'Oh, hello!' The Prime Minister stood up, now wearing his familiar smile. 'It's Rebecca, isn't it?'

'You haven't answered my question. Are you

responsible for this?'

'Well, I, er...'

She took hold of the hilt of the sword that had remained by her side throughout.

'Look, Rebecca, we really don't know exactly what happened yet, but I've already started a full inquiry by asking Lord Anthem here what he thinks.'

The Prime Minister then looked at Lord Anthem and asked, 'Non quod iustum est?'

'Yes, that's right, Robert, but as I've just been telling you, I can't see how even you will be able to cover up what is clearly an unprovoked shelling of a thousand people who'd been doing nothing more dangerous than having a picnic! And if you try, you'll then have to explain to the press why HMS Britannica was forced to launch her Sea Dart missiles and turn an entire battalion of three hundred army personnel, and a general, into what now looks like a giant tin of exploded dog food.'

A bead of sweat rolled innocently down the Prime Minister's forehead, but that was the only sign of him feeling the pressure as he just continued to smile with gay abandon.

'Look, Reggie, why don't you pop down to Number 10 for lunch tomorrow and we can chat about it then. In fact,' and he turned to beam over at Rebecca, 'why don't you both come down? You can bring some of your Roman chums as well! I'm sure that if we all sit down together, we can soon have this whole tragic affair smoothed over.'

Rebecca was about to run him through with her sword, right there and then. At that precise moment she thought that not only would she be doing her country a favour, but she would probably be knighted for making the effort. But just as she was about to unsheathe it, she had an even better idea.

Taking her hand off the hilt she answered, 'Thank you, Prime Minister. That really is very generous of you. We'd love to come down, but maybe not until the weekend. I think we'll need just a little more time to get back on our feet, probably with the help of a few good surgeons and some NHS Zimmer frames.'

She spoke with as much sincerity as she could muster, but was unable to keep the sarcasm from her voice.

The Prime Minister looked at her with some suspicion, not sure if she was being serious, but he'd made the offer in good faith and thought that as long as they all left their swords with the policeman outside his front door, he couldn't see a problem.

'Well, that's settled then,' he said with a great show of delight. 'Lunch on Saturday at my place. I'll send a helicopter for you at, what, say eleven? My secretary will sort out the details. Cheerio and see you then!' and spread his smile around again before returning to the ongoing meeting with the Government's Creative Writing Team, who'd managed to come up with what they believed to be a winning story that needed his approval. Apparently, a British general had gone completely mad, launching an unprovoked attack on a local parade before, wracked with guilt, blowing himself up along with a battalion of Royal Artillery using a hidden munitions dump he'd buried there a few weeks earlier.

When the PM was out of ear shot, Lord Anthem turned to Rebecca.

'So, what exactly have you got up your sleeve, young lady?'

She winked at him. 'Oh, nothing much, but I don't see why we can't take our PM for a trip to the cleaners before calling it a day; and anyway, it would be nice to see inside Number 10. I'd also like to take Inspector Capstan down, the policeman we ran over on Saturday. I can't help but feel sorry for him; after all, he was only doing his job and the card I sent him was probably a little harsh.

'Very well, my dear, as long as you know what you're doing; but just be careful. The Prime Minister's a powerful man and there's not a lot he can't do with a phone and access to his email.'

'Yes, I'm sure you're right, but that's exactly what I'm counting on!'

CHAPTER XXXII
QUID EST VERITAS?
What is truth?

HAVING BEEN GIVEN clearance to pass through the wrought iron gates that defend Downing Street against the threat of Al-Qaeda and disgruntled nurses, Rebecca led her party towards the famous polished black door that awaited them about half way down. She had to admit to feeling both nervous and excited. Even she couldn't help but be moved by the occasion, and as she made her way along the quaint London street wearing her brand new white cotton tunic dress and holding a smaller than normal handbag, both of which she'd picked up from M&S, she started to look for the correct door number before remembering that it was the one with the policeman standing outside, and the small group of paparazzi opposite.

Besides Rebecca marched Lord Reginald Anthem, and they were followed by Mark, Doughnut, Sebastian, Johnno, Captain Blankard and Lieutenant Haffinger. Rebecca had insisted that they all attend, even if it did mean two helicopters were needed. They'd all played their part and so deserved to be rewarded with lunch at Number 10.

However, Rebecca wasn't really leading the procession, as she was pushing Inspector Capstan in front of her, still wheelchair-bound having suffered two broken legs, a fractured arm, cracked ribs, and a broken jaw. And hobbling on crutches beside him was Sergeant Dewbush, who'd somehow managed to escape with just a twisted ankle and mild concussion.

As they reached the glossy door, the jolly-looking policemen knocked twice to alert the security guard inside to open up. Rebecca lifted the front wheels of Capstan's wheelchair over the first shallow step and then up again to clear the door's sill, before pushing him all the way inside.

As they entered they were greeted by the Prime Minister's Private Secretary, Fredrick Overtoun, who guided them through to the formal dining room that had been laid out for a feast, and as they navigated themselves around to their labelled seats, Lord Anthem asked, 'Will the PM be joining us?'

'He certainly hopes to,' replied Fredrick, 'but he's had to take an urgent call from Brussels. Something to do with the price of German sausage meat and how it may impact the Pound. But he has asked me to apologise for his tardiness and to continue in his absence. There's wine on the table and I'll have your starters brought straight in.'

Rebecca remembered something.

'Oh, can we have a straw for Inspector Capstan, please? He's still struggling to eat solid food,' and patted his head as though he were a dog.

Capstan had become used to being petted like man's best friend, and although he still held a certain amount of resentment towards his former nemesis, she'd been treating him like royalty all day and, to an extent, he had been swayed by her abundance of natural charm. So, as Fredrick left to find him a straw, he leaned over to Rebecca who now sat by his side and said, 'Ank ou eggecca,' which was about the best he could do without moving his still wired-up jaw. Over the last two weeks he'd become reasonably proficient at talking with just the back of his tongue, so much so that he'd bought himself the book, "Ventriloquism for Dummies" from Amazon. It had certainly helped him while away the long hours as he convalesced in hospital, and had also given him a new use for his redundant socks, which had made excellent makeshift puppets.

Sitting on Rebecca's left-hand side was Lord Anthem who whispered to her, 'I doubt we'll be seeing our PM until afterwards. He's not known for joining his more "common" guests for lunch and always makes up some excuse involving the price of German sausage meat. He's probably in the garden, practicing his golf swing.'

But Rebecca really didn't care. She hadn't come all that way to lunch with the Prime Minister, only to talk to him, in private, and as long as he made himself available afterwards, she was more than happy to enjoy the company of the many new friends she'd made during that long and highly entertaining summer. And as she sat there, listening to the banter and sampling the soup, her mind drifted towards her final plan, that of not having to return to Bath, her various part-time jobs or her final year's Business Degree course. She had new horizons in mind and hoped to be enjoying them from the deck of a large yacht moored opposite her cliff top villa, somewhere off the coast of Italy.

And so it was that, after about an hour of wining, dining and battle scar posturing, the coffee and cigars were brought in and Fredrick Overtoun rested a hand on Rebecca's shoulder and said, 'The Prime Minister is ready to see you now.'

Nodding, she retrieved her freshly poured coffee and stood up to say, 'Would you all please excuse me for a few minutes?' and followed Fredrick out.

She was led down a narrow hallway to a door where Fredrick knocked before entering.

'Rebecca of Bath is here to see you now, Prime Minister.'

Fredrick then ushered her inside and closed the door on his way out.

'Rebecca, Rebecca, Rebecca,' the Prime Minister said, placing his seven iron back into the golf bag beside his desk. 'I'm so glad you could come.'

'It's my pleasure, Prime Minister.'

'And I'm most awfully sorry I couldn't join you for lunch but I had Brussels on the phone, banging on about the price of pork.'

He then removed his golf glove and said, 'Do please have a seat.'

'Thank you, Prime Minister,' and made her way over to the sumptuous red leather arm chair in the corner to which he gestured.

Making herself comfortable, she took a sip from her coffee before placing it down on the antique Georgian coffee table beside her. Robert, meanwhile, picked up a newspaper from his desk and strolled over to the chair opposite.

Now that she was actually sitting beside the Prime Minister, in his own office, at Number 10, she was surprised at just how calm she felt. She was expecting to be nervous and intimidated, but it was not the case. She knew exactly what she wanted from the meeting and, having avoided the red wine served during lunch, she still had a clear head and a single-minded purpose.

'Did you see the papers?' asked Robert, with his familiar, genial smile, and offered her the one he now held.

It was a copy of The Sun, from a few days earlier, but as she hadn't seen it, or any other newspaper, since what the media had called, "The Battle of Bath", she accepted it and gave the front page a courtesy glance.

"BARMY ARMY COMMITS HARI KARI".

The accompanying photograph was an aerial shot of the crater left by the two Sea Dart missiles.

She didn't bother to read the rest and folded it before placing it down beside her coffee.

'Yes, most amusing, Prime Minister, but unfortunately we both know that that isn't exactly true, now is it?'

Robert leaned back in his chair and crossed his legs.

'Who am I to say what is true or not?' and he spread his arms out like Caesar, addressing his Senate. 'In this age in which we live, the media says what it says, and the rest of the world believes it. A better question would probably be, "Quid est veritas?"'

Rebecca had no idea what that meant, but wasn't about to show intellectual weakness by asking.

'I completely agree with you, Prime Minister, which is why I, personally, never watch or read the news. But I am aware that most people do, and that their views and opinions are easily swayed by it.'

'So you understand your position then? All the newspapers this week have been running the story that General Hillander-Moss went completely mad, leaving behind a large crater as his only legacy. Even the F.T.

went with the story and followed it up by saying that our country needs to invest in more sophisticated weaponry to help make it a safer place for visiting nations.'

'Again, I completely agree with you, Prime Minister. It would seem that the power of the media cannot be underestimated.'

Robert was now looking at her through narrowing eyes, as he tried to calculate exactly what it was that she was up to. He'd never knowingly underestimated anyone, and wasn't about to start with this provocative young lady.

'So, may I ask what it is that you'd like to talk about?'

'Oh, I just wanted to let you know what I'm going to be up to for the next couple of weeks. I've been surprised by the amount of interest the press has shown in me, so I've agreed to give a couple of interviews.'

The PM may not have been the sharpest stick in Parliament, but he knew where this was going.

'And may I ask which newspapers you've been talking to?'

'As I said, just one or two.'

'Oh, do feel free to name them.'

Robert knew exactly which papers he needed to be concerned about.

'The Daily Bath have said that they'd like to run a story about me.'

And that wasn't one of them.

'As would The Bristol Beagle.'

Neither was that.

'Any more?' he asked, hoping that this was where

her ambition ended.

'Well, on Monday I've agreed to do a photoshoot with The Sun, who'd like me as their new Page Three Girl. They're also keen to run a series of "Kiss and Tell" stories that mainly involve you and your frequent visits to my Boudoir of Pain, over in Bath. They've given it the working title of, "PM Bangs Bath Beauty", which I quite like. I'm fairly sure your wife and children would appreciate it as well. I'm also doing a centre page spread in both Penthouse and Playboy on Thursday and Friday, alongside similar articles, but aimed more at their international readership. OK Magazine has asked to run a story about how you and I were kicked out of a London hotel for enjoying both excessive copulation and cocaine during a cheese and orange juice party given by some famous Arab sheikh, whose name escapes me. That interview is due to take place next Monday. And the Financial Times would like to run a story about how you paid me a million pounds to have your old university chum, General Hillander-Moss, blown up along with three hundred British soldiers, simply because he slept with your daughter, who's just turned fifteen, I believe. However, when I do meet with them I'm most definitely going to say, in your defence, that the only reason he did have sex with your daughter was because you had sex with his twelve year-old one first, We haven't scheduled a date for that yet, but their Editor in Chief, a Charles Grousehill, who I believe you know, says he's free a week on Tuesday.'

As this woman continued to outline her itinerary for the next couple of weeks, Robert began to feel increasingly nauseous, and with his well-rehearsed grin becoming more like that of a stone gargoyle overlooking an old church graveyard, in a remote corner of Northumberland, at midnight, on Halloween, he forced himself to ask, 'And is there anyone else you've been talking to?'

'As it happens, yes! I've also been contacted by a publishing house who have a ghost writer standing by, ready to write my memoirs. I must admit that this is the one I'm most excited about. The book's going to be called, "Rebecca of Bath, the Slaughtered Virgin of Zenopolis", but is mostly going to feature you, your daughter, Hillander-Moss, his daughter and a Catholic girls' boarding school which you both used as a venue for a series of underage sex parties.'

Robert had heard enough. This girl clearly had no bounds to her imagination which, in political terms, made her the most dangerous person in the UK, so he cut to the chase.

'So, what is it exactly that you'd like from me?'

'Well, as you know I don't really care much for the media. I am, at heart, a private person; however, they're all offering me rather large sums of money, which it's proving difficult to decline.'

She paused for dramatic effect.

'Go on.'

'So, instead of going down the international celebrity route, I'd like to win the Lottery.'

'Well, you'd better buy yourself a ticket then!' he said with a nervous laugh.

Rebecca just stared at him.

'I really don't know what you expect me to do about that, I'm not God or anything!'

She continued to glare.

'Look, honestly, I can't predict lottery numbers. It's just not possible!'

The room fell into an oppressive silence.

'Very well! How much do you want to win?'

'Ten million.'

'But can't I just give that to you? It would be a lot easier. I can have the money transferred over to your account first thing Monday morning.'

'Yes, but it would be very difficult for me to explain to the tax man where all that money came from, and I can't be bothered to open a Swiss bank account. And I also suspect that such a large sum would attract the attention of the Fraud Squad, and I don't wish to be looking over my shoulder for the rest of my life. No, I just want to win the Lottery, fair and square. Then I can buy a villa in Italy with a decent view over the Med and enjoy the rest of my life without having to wear quite so many clothes all the time.'

'Very well. Is that it?'

'No! I want Inspector Capstan to be awarded an OBE and be given a decent pay rise. He deserves that for having the courage to stand up to me.'

'OK, agreed. Anything else?'

'I'd like Sergeant Dewbush to be given a lifetime subscription to Spank n' Wank magazine. I think he'd enjoy that.'

Robert was beginning to think that he should have brought a pen.

'Is there anything else?'

'Yes. I'd like the Roman Imperialists to receive Sport England funding.'

'But, from what I understand, they're a battle re-enactment group. I don't think they'd qualify.'

'I'm coming to that. I'd also like it to become an Olympic sport.'

'You'd like what to become an Olympic sport?'

'Battle Re-enactment! It really is great fun and I think it will solve a lot of the world's problems if countries could feel as if they really were going to war, without actually doing so.'

She had a good point, and Robert made a mental note to add it to his manifesto.

'Anything else?' he asked.

'No, that's it.'

'And if I give you all those things, then you'll forget about the whole Battle of Bath incident?'

'If you meet all my requirements, then I'll be moving to Italy and you'll never hear from me again.'

He wrapped his fingers together and pretended to deliberate over the matter, but secretly he was delighted. Not only was the whole affair going to leave his personal bank account untouched, but she did seem to be rather keen to leave the country, and just as soon as she did, he'd have her passport revoked.

'And if you do decide to relate your story to any journalist, in any part of the world, you do realise that I'd be forced to seek a more permanent solution to your continued existence.'

Rebecca gave him a cold hard stare. She wasn't in the least bit fazed by his unveiled threat.

'And you do realise that if you don't give me what I want, I'll raise another Roman army that will make the last one look like a junior school's production of Julius Caesar. And with it I'll re-take Britain, make Buckingham Palace my new home and turn this place into a stable.'

Having heard from Lord Anthem how she'd being able to recruit two thousand men for a simple parade, he wasn't prepared to doubt her intent, but she hadn't finished.

'And that's after I've become a famous international celebrity and made sure you're locked up for mass murder, bribery and child abuse.'

He'd had enough. She was just too dangerous, even by his standards, so he stood up and said, 'Right then, we're agreed!' and put his hand out.

As he stood, so did she, and looked down at his offered hand before shaking it.

'Splendid, splendid, splendid,' said Robert, and strode over to the office door. 'Now, let me see you back to your chums and I'll start making some calls.'

'Thank you, Prime Minister. It's been a pleasure.'

'No, really, the pleasure's been all mine,' and he pulled open the door to see Fredrick waiting outside.

'Ah, there you are, Freddy. Could you please escort Rebecca back to her friends? It would seem that I have some more work to do.'

'Of course, Prime Minister. If you could follow me please, Rebecca, I'll return you to the dining room and have some fresh coffee brought in.'

CHAPTER XXXIII
Q.E.D.
QUOD ERAT DEMONSTRANDUM
Which is what had to be proven

BY THE TIME they emerged from Number 10, word had got out that Rebecca of Bath was visiting the Prime Minister, and there was now an impressive bevy of boisterous paparazzi waiting for them outside, whose fully charged cameras erupted with a dazzling display that would have gone well with Tchaikovsky's 1812 Overture in E♭ major.

'Rebecca, over here Rebecca!'
'Oi! Rebecca! Give us a smile?'
'Did you meet the Prime Minister, Rebecca?'
'What did you talk about?'
'Where's your sword?'
'Where's your army?'
'Have you got a helmet?'
'Did he run you a bath?'
'How about a basin?'
'Did you have a bath with him?'
'Did you have sex with him in the bath?'
'Did you have sex with him in the bath and then go for a swim in a basin?'
'Have you ever swum with a dolphin?'

'Have you ever had sex with one?'

'Have you ever had sex with a dolphin whilst having a bath with the Prime Minister?'

'Have you ever had sex with a dolphin and the Prime Minister whilst having a bath before going for a swim in a basin?'

But by the time the questions had reached these new heights of absurdity, Rebecca's group was already half way down the street and, thankfully, just out of ear shot. Once back out through the wrought iron gates, they said farewell to Lord Anthem, Captain Blankard and Lieutenant Haffinger, who had to get back to their various ports of call, leaving the remaining group to take a stroll over towards Buckingham Palace to try to catch the Changing of the Guard.

On the way there, unimpressed with Capstan's mastery of the dark mystical art that is Ventriloquism, they popped in to a newsagent's to buy him some paper and a felt tip pen, so that he could write down whatever it was that he wanted to say.

And as they now gathered outside another impressive black wrought iron gate, which seemed to be all the rage in London, they gazed through the railings towards the Queen's main residence, trying to spot her through one of the many windows having a cup of tea.

With everyone now preoccupied, Rebecca pulled out the brand new smartphone that had been a special gift from Lord Anthem, courtesy of MI6. She didn't trust the Prime Minister as far as she could push him against a wall with a sharpened spear, and as she hadn't lined up a single interview, with a single newspaper or magazine, and had no intention of doing so, she'd requested the use of the most sophisticated bugging device on the market to give her a little more leverage. It was that miniscule covert gadget that she'd been able to smuggle in to Number 10 using Capstan's wheelchair as a clandestine carrier, and it was that bug that she'd planted under the antique Georgian coffee table where they'd had their little chat, to record their conversation and all those he had afterwards and until such a time as it was discovered.

Tapping on the specially installed app that was merrily recording every sound and syllable that emanated from his office, she placed the phone against her ear and listened.

In the background she could clearly hear him, chatting away on the phone.

'I don't give a fuck what you're the Archbishop of! If you don't find a way to stop those school girls talking to everyone they know about those bloody sex parties, I'll most definitely find a way to get your pretty little choir boys on to Crimewatch, along with a graphic video reconstruction and an appeal for information relating to the whereabouts of an old man with a big stick and a pointy hat. Can't you force them to take a vow of silence or something? How about locking them up in a convent up north somewhere?'

Smiling to herself she checked that it was still recording before placing it back into her handbag. Then she heard Capstan mumbling with excitement and gesticulating at the palace before he scrawled out, "THE QUEEN!" in capitals and pointed again.

'That's nice, dear,' she said and patted him on the head.

Then she too gazed over at the vast ornate building,

thinking that it could make quite a nice home, but was probably rather irksome to keep clean. Maybe if the PM didn't keep his promise, and if the mood took her, it could be fun to invade London.

But summer was drawing to an end and the British winter had never suited her. Anyway, she'd already spoken to an agent in Italy about a good-sized estate with an olive tree plantation. She really fancied herself as a wealthy Italian land owner and, at that moment, had just thought of what she considered to be the perfect name for what she'd like to produce. And with that in mind she asked Capstan if she could borrow his pen and paper, and then wrote down, "Slaughtered Virgin Olive Oil." Then she looked at it from arm's reach and a wide grin spread over her face. It may be that the word "Slaughtered" could put people off, and that she'd be better off opening a butcher's, but chopping up horses to make ready meals really wasn't her thing. No, olive oil was the way forward, and if that failed, she could always accept the offer of becoming a British Spy that had come with the bugging device: which reminded her…

She gave the paper and pen back to Capstan and pulled out her smartphone again to do a quick Google search for the next flight out of London. There was already a chill in the air and she had no intention of buying another bloody jumper.

THE SLAUGHTERED VIRGIN OF ZENOPOLIS

ABOUT THE AUTHOR

HAVING BEEN BORN in a US Navy hospital in California, David spent the first eight years of his life being transported from one country to another, before ending up in a three bedroom semi-detached house in Devon, on the South Coast of England.

David's Father, a devout Navy Commander, and his Mother, a loyal Christian missionary, then decided to pack him off to an all-boys boarding school in Surrey, where they thought it would be fun for him to take up ballet. Once there, he showed a remarkable aptitude for dance and, being the only boy in the school to learn, found numerous opportunities to demonstrate the many and varied movements he'd been taught, normally whilst fending off attacks from his classroom chums who seemed unable to appreciate the skill required to turn around in circles, without falling over.

Meanwhile, his Father began to push him down the more regimented path towards becoming a trained assassin, and spent the school holidays teaching him how to use an air rifle. Over the years, and with his Father's expert tuition, he became a proficient marksman, managing to shoot a number of things directly in the head. His most common targets were birds but also extended to those less obvious, including his brother, sister, an uncle who popped in for tea, and several un-suspecting neighbours caught doing some gardening.

Horrified by the prospect of her youngest son spending his adult life travelling the world to indiscriminately kill people, for no particular reason, his Mother intensified her efforts for him to enter the more highbrow world of the theatre by applying him to enter for the Royal Ballet. But after his twenty minute audition, during which time he jumped and twirled just as high and as fast as he possibly could, the three ballet aficionados who'd stared at him throughout with unhidden incredulity, proclaimed to his proud Mother that the best and only role they could offer him would be that of, "Third Tree from the Left" during their next performance of Pinocchio, but that would involve him being cut down, with an axe, during the opening scene. Furthermore, they'd be unable to guarantee his safety as the director had decided to use a real axe instead of the normal foam rubber one, to add to the drama of an otherwise rather staid production.

A few weeks later, and unable to find any suitable life insurance, David's Mother gave up her dream for him to become a famed Primo Ballerino and left him to his own devices.

And so it was, that with a sense of freedom little before known, he enrolled himself at a local college to study Chain Smoking, Under-Age Drinking, Drug Abuse and Fornication but forgot all about his core academic subjects. Subsequently he failed his 'A' Levels and moved to live in a tent in Dorking where he picked up with his more practised skills whilst working as a Barbed Wire Fencer.

Having being able to survive the hurricane of '87, the one that took down every tree within a fifty mile radius of his tent, he felt blessed, and must have been destined for greater things, other than sleeping rough during the night and being repeatedly stabbed by hard to control pieces of metal during the day. So he talked his way onto a Business Degree Course at the University of Southampton.

After three years of intensive study and to the surprise of just about everyone, he graduated with a 2:1 and spent the next ten years working in several incomprehensibly depressing sales jobs in Central London, before setting up his own recruitment firm.

Seven highly profitable years later, during which time he married and had two children, the Credit Crunch hit, which ended that particular episode of his career.

It's at this point he decided to become a writer which is where you find him now, happily married and living in London with his young family.

When not writing he spends his time attempting to persuade his wife that she really doesn't need to buy the entire contents of Ikea, even if there is a sale on. And when there are no items of flat-packed furniture for him to assemble he enjoys writing, base-jumping, and drawing up plans to demolish his house to build the world's largest charity shop.

www.david-blake.com

Printed in Great Britain
by Amazon